Love Looks Back

The Search for Siblings

C. A. Simonson

Book II of the Journey Home Series

Cover Design by C.A. Simonson
All scripture quotations are taken from the Holy Bible
King James Version, public domain.

Published by Aspen Run Press

Copyright © 2015 C.A. Simonson
All rights reserved.
ISBN-13: 978-1511555081
ISBN-10: 1511555084

ACKNOWLEDGMENTS

I am grateful to my husband who has been a great collaborator with his listening ear, helpful suggestions, and springboard of ideas for this book.
He has encouraged me to pursue my dream of writing.

I thank Toni Somers, a dear friend and colleague of Springfield Writers Guild, who was a great encouragement in the writing of this book and helped with the editing. I am also grateful to the other beta readers who were kind enough to give their suggestions and thoughts.

.

Table of Contents

Chapter 1 - Reflection

Dolores Ryan caught her breath in between stitches as she hemmed the little dress in her lap. Pain forced tears to her eyes. Her cramps were becoming more consistent, and it worried her. It was too early.

She pinned the needle to the dress and set it in the basket. Dol leaned back in her sewing rocker for a much-needed breather. She rubbed her swollen belly which seemed to get larger by the day. Dol enjoyed her afternoon quiet time while the girls slept. It gave her time to mend, and time to think and reflect. She checked the clock and looked out the front window. Benny would be home from work soon.

Dear, sweet Benny. How she loved her man. He was her rock. He took good care of her and allowed her to work her business out of their home. She was grateful for her husband, and she loved the beautiful country home he provided for her and her family. Settled off the roads and nestled in the trees, it gave a sense of seclusion and security although they were only a few miles from town.

Another cramp caught her off guard, making her dizzy and lightheaded. Her thoughts went to her own mother who met an early death with her eighth child.

Ma worked so hard and did so much for us. I did as much as I could to help with the little ones, but I couldn't be there when she really needed me. Don't know why I'm so emotional these days. Dol put her head in her hands and let the tears flow.

Four-year-old Lizzie cupped her chubby hands under her mother's chin and lifted it toward hers. "What's the matter, Mama? Why are you crying?"

Dol wiped her face with her apron and smiled at her daughter. "Oh, it's nothing, Lizzie. Mama's just thinking about some things. What are you doing out of bed already?"

Lizzie put her hands on her hips and pursed her lips. "Well, I'm hungry," she stated as a matter of fact. "Besides, baby Molly is fussin'. She woke me up."

"Well, it's time to get up anyway. I suppose the baby is hungry too."

Dol struggled to rise from her rocker, holding her back as she got up. This one is sure sitting differently. She rubbed at the bulge of her belly as she picked up her sewing basket.

Your Papa will be home soon, Missy. I better get supper ready."

"Can I help?"

"Of course you can." Dol smiled at the youngster. "Go fetch me four potatoes from the bin."

"Okay, Mama," Lizzie grinned and ran off toward the root cellar.

Baby Molly squealed with delight as she saw her mother enter the room. She clapped her little hands and held them up, searching her mother's eyes with her own.

"Aren't you the happy one?" Dol picked her up and gave her a squeeze. "And I'm sure you'll be even happier when I change you."

Dol changed the baby's diaper and then lifted the child from the crib. She felt a sharp twinge in her lower abdomen, forcing her to stop short. It's nothing, she told herself. She carried Molly to the kitchen and set her in her highchair and then began to prepare supper.

"Here you go, Mama." Lizzie dropped the potatoes from her dress held to make a basket. "What next?"

Dol laughed. "So eager to please, you are, my little Miss. Go grab some carrots."

So much energy. She rubbed her belly as the baby gave another hard kick. And I am so blessed. Another child, another life given from above. Make this one healthy, Lord.

This pregnancy was harder. The first trimester was filled with constant nausea and not just morning sickness. She always felt queasy. The first two pregnancies had gone smoothly, but this child was different. Maybe he was the boy her husband wanted the first two times. He said they would keep trying until he got one. It made Dol smile.

Her mother bore seven babies...and died with the eighth. I wonder if she had problems with all her babies. Never said anything, but I guess that isn't something a mother would tell a twelve-year-old.

Gracie, the baby of our family, would be a teenager by now. Wonder if she and Josie are still together? Would I even recognize them?

Dol shook her head. Her mind trailed to the past once more as she thought of that freezing night ten years before when she and her siblings sat on the crooked, wooden fence waiting for their Pa to come home. It had been a cold, miserable night with rain, wind, and then sleet.

Dolores Louise Larue was second born in the Larue family of seven, named after her great-grandmother. She had a mother's heart for her younger siblings – Frankie, Mikie, the twins: Josie and Jesse, and Gracie – all one to two years apart in age. Her mother depended on her to help with the younger children, especially after the twins were born, although she was only eight years old.

She thought of poor Gracie, so tiny and frail at

four years of age, being hung by her coat to the post because she couldn't balance enough to sit on top. Dolly finally had to make the choice to rescue her little sister and defy Pa's orders to stay on the fence, but she didn't care. Gracie's cries in the cold icy rain had become too much to bear. Dolly had to do something and was willing to bear the consequences. Gracie may have frozen some fingers or worse had Dolly not helped her down and warmed her up. She was glad big brother Guy made the hard decision to escape to the barn for the night. It was a good thing they did. Their father never did come back that night, and they were left to figure out what to do.

Ma taught her how to cook and help the children learn to read and write. After Ma died, the weight of cooking, cleaning, and caring for the children fell on her shoulders.

I tried hard too, Dol mused as she peeled potatoes. Pa made it really hard to feed a big family when he drank all the grocery money away. Dol felt the blood rise in her face as the scene made her angry all over again. He was always drinking the money away and then beating on Ma or Guy. I'm almost glad Ma died, she confessed to herself and then was shocked at her awful thought. At least she got away.

Dol dug a pot out of the cupboard and filled it

with water for the potatoes. Molly banged the highchair tray with her hands and squealed.

"Yes, little one. You are next. I won't forget to feed you." Dol dropped a few crackers on the tray to keep the child satisfied for a few minutes while she prepared the baby's food.

"Here's the carrots. What else can I do Mama?"

"You're a love, Lizzie. You've helped Mama a lot, and I love you so much." She kissed Lizzie's forehead. "Now go greet your Papa. I hear him coming up the drive." She is the same age as Gracie when we all parted ways.

Dol's heart had been broken the morning they separated, but she drove away the tears; she couldn't let her baby sisters see her crying. No. She had to be strong for them.

The older boys would be okay. They could take care of themselves. Frankie was told to go to Farmer Wheeler's to see if he could pawn his muscles for some room and board. Guy planned to take the two younger boys to the Johnsons. He hoped they would find a place in their family for Mikie and Jesse. She trusted it all worked out...but guessed she would never know.

Guy told Dolly to take the girls to the preacher's and tell him their story. She was to ask if he would help them find a place to live. Dol had hoped it would be easy. She wanted to find the girls a wonderful family to live with.

She wanted the same for her brothers. She had lost touch with every one of them, and the sadness overwhelmed her.

C.A. Simonson

Chapter 2 - Going Back

Frank Larue was weary from the ten hour drive back to his hometown of Tekamah, Nebraska, north of Omaha. He swore he would never return. Too many bad memories. There were good times too, he had to admit.

Before checking into the hotel, he decided to drive out to the old homestead. Tomorrow was Saturday. The weekend would give him plenty of time to look around, visit some landmarks, and see if anyone remembered his siblings or knew of their whereabouts.

The old town hadn't changed much. The one room schoolhouse was now a museum. The doc's office had become a small clinic.

From town, he headed west along Old Tree Lane where tall cottonwoods guarded either side of the road. Past Mill Pond, the stately Johnson homestead still guarded its place on the corner. Frank felt a hard pit beginning to form in his stomach. He turned the car north and passed the Wheeler farm where he lived for five years. Mac, although old enough to be his grandfather, was like a father to him. He learned a lot from the old man and many more painful lessons from his missus. Wondered if he or his missus were still alive. Mac's old farmhouse looked vacant. He decided to ask in town.

Almost at the old homestead, he slowed with the thought of turning around. Why did I come back? He gritted his teeth and drove the car up the old dirt road toward the shack they used to call home. He parked the car and scanned the area. Memories flooded back from his childhood.

The barn didn't look much better than the shack. Faded and broken siding hung lopsided in places, allowing sun, rain, and critters to enter. Weeds and grass had grown up around the edges adding to the abandoned look of the old place.

Frank paused inside the barn door. Old moldy bales made the air stale; hay lay strewn about the floor. He recalled the icy cold October night when he and his siblings decided to sleep in the barn to escape the sleet. How tired, cold, and achy they all were and needed warmth and sleep. They all wondered where their Pa had disappeared to. It was a mystery.

"Why is he taking so long? Did something happen to him? Why did he leave us? What will we do if Pa doesn't come back?" were questions they all wanted answered.

His brothers and sisters stuck together. Little

Gracie cuddled close against her older sister, Dolly. Josie was snug and secure under Dolly's other arm. Dolly was so much like Mama. Dolly loved and cared for us all, especially her little sisters. He recalled the salty tears that rolled down her freckled cheeks. Wonder where his sisters wound up? The preacher will know. I must find my sisters and brother again.

Waves of guilt, pain, and sorrow swept over Frank. Little brother Jesse, only six years old, died not long after we left this dirty place. Jesse coughed on and off all night. The dust in the hay or air may be what made him so sick.

He looked toward the high window in the haymow. Big brother Guy searched the road for hours seeking for some sign of Pa's return. Guy knew he was in charge whether he liked it or not, even though he was only fourteen. He knew he had to find a way out for all of us. We knew he had the final say and that was okay. Guy was a good brother. Bulky muscles made him strong from work in the field, and he was smart; he knew we would be safe and warm in the barn.

Wonder where he went? Did he ever find Pa? He promised he'd bring us all back together if he did. Maybe he found something he didn't want us to know.

Frank turned to leave the barn with a heavy

heart. One more place to check before he left the homestead – not that he wanted to – he had to: the gravesite behind the barn.

He stood by the barn door and looked across the barren field beyond. Waves of emotion and sorrow washed over him. Strange, Pa never told us what happened to Mama and the baby. Guess we just figured it out. I'm glad she was taken from this miserable life. She didn't deserve the life she had.

Pa stuck two crude crosses made with sticks and baling twine in the mounds of dirt behind the barn. The huge mounds he remembered at age ten had been worn away by the elements. As Frank got closer, he was taken back. He knew of Mama's and the baby's graves, but no more. So, why are there three crosses?

Troubled, he went to examine the third cross. A small folded wad of paper was nailed to it. He carefully pried it off. Faded, the almost illegible words read, "LEROY LARUE."

With shaky hands he opened the folded paper, and a shiver went up his spine.

"FOUND HIM. BURIED HIM. SMW"

Chapter 3 - Alarm

Ben snuck up behind his wife and wrapped his arms around her protruding belly.

"Where are you, Dol?" The child within kicked his hand. He patted the spot and then kissed Dol on her neck. "Are you in another world?"

Dol jumped as he touched her. She hadn't realized she'd been staring out the kitchen window for the last few minutes engrossed in the past. "Oh, Benny. You scared me. I didn't even hear you come in. Just deep in thought, that's all."

"Everything okay?"

She leaned into his embrace. "Sure. I'm fine. It's nothing." Subconsciously, she rubbed at the sore spot on her lower back.

He gave her another kiss on her neck and rubbed the spot where she had put her hand. "Baby boy's jumpy today, huh?"

"Boy? You're so sure, are you?" she giggled.

"I can hope. Well, supper smells delicious, Sweets. Sure glad I won the bet when I got you." He winked.

Dol gave Ben a little push and giggled again. "Benny Ryan! I'm surprised you'd think of that now," she patted his face. "You always know how to cheer me up. Go relax now. Supper is almost ready. I'll call you when it's done."

Ben turned to leave the room when he heard Dol gasp for breath. He whirled around in time to catch her before she sunk to the floor.

"Dol!" Alarm sounded in his voice, "What's wrong?"

Dol grasped her belly as another searing pain coursed through her body. "The baby...Benny. Help..." she gasped again, "it's...too...soon." She started to sob.

"Don't worry, Sweets. I'll take care of you," Ben's insides quaked. It *was* too soon. She still has close to two months to go. He led her to the couch.

"Benny..." her eyes brimmed with tears and pain, "take me to the hospital. Now. The baby's coming."

It shook Ben to see her eyes wild with fear, her face wracked with pain. He was flustered – something which didn't happen often. A well-trained lawyer with full control of his inner emotions, he couldn't afford to be rattled, but this was an area out of his control, out of his territory. All he knew was he had to take care of his wife and it had to be quick. It was too early for the baby to be born, but she did seem to be in labor. He ought to know these signs after two births. He kept his voice calm, his demeanor soft. He didn't want to alarm her any more than necessary.

"I will call Mama Vi. We can drop the girls off there on the way to the hospital."

"Hurry, Benny," Dol yelped as another pain gripped her. "Please. Hurry."

Almost as soon as Dol was settled into her hospital bed, the pains stopped. Ben parked the car and rushed toward her room. He met the doctor in the hallway, who followed him into Dol's room.

"Nothing but false labor, Mr. Ryan. I would like her to stay overnight so we can keep an eye on her, just in case," said the doctor.

Relieved, Ben walked into his wife's room where she sat up in bed with a sheepish grin.

"I feel so foolish, Benny. All that trouble for nothing. I should know by now what real labor pains feel like."

"Shhh... It's okay, Sweets. It never hurts to be on the safe side. Besides, maybe you just need a good night's sleep without worrying over the children or me."

"I'm just a worrier, you know?"

Ben nodded. Yes. He knew. They had been through this with their first two children. Dolly imagined herself dying like her mother each time, and it frightened her to wits' end. Their first child, Elizabeth Vi, was no problem at all. The pregnancy went smoothly throughout the nine months despite Dolly's worry. Molly Lou came along a couple years later and was also a normal pregnancy and birth.

This pregnancy was different, he had to admit. Different in every way. The first three months Dolly was violently nauseous, in her second trimester her digestive system settled down, but she began to spot and worried constantly about losing the baby. As the child grew–and seemed to grow fast–her belly swelled making her think of her mother often. The doctor always insisted there was nothing to worry about. Spotting could be normal.

"I'm glad I have you, Benny. You're my rock," Dol continued oblivious to Ben's thoughts.

Yes. He knew the story well, but he was concerned too. This child was a fighter. Maybe I'll get me my son yet, he mused. He smiled inwardly as he rubbed his wife's back.

"You know I'm here for you, Dol. You rest tonight, hear? Listen to the doctor. He'll take good care of you. Don't worry about Lizzie and Molly. They'll be just fine. I'll be back to pick you up in the morning."

Dol reached up as Ben lowered his face to kiss her good night. "Thanks, Benny. I love you."

"You're my sweet love," he whispered back, as he stroked her hair away from her face. "You rest now. I'll be back tomorrow. Promise."

Dol smiled and waved goodbye. How she loved her man. She snuggled under the warm covers and rubbed her belly. "Well, little guy, you definitely want to make a grand entrance, don't you? Help your mama out now, and behave tonight. Let me get some rest." She smiled, and dreamed of having the son her husband always wanted. The girls' pregnancies were so different; this one just had to be a boy.

Chapter 4 - Sad News

Early Saturday morning, Frank began his day at Fanny's Corner Café – the same place Mr. Simmons had taken him years before; the place Frank heard the cockamamie story of Simmons being his biological father. Frank bit his lip. Uneasiness settled over him as he found a booth in the opposite corner of the one he once shared with Mr. Simmons.

I came to put things behind me; to conquer my past. That's what Anne wants me to do. That's what I need to do. He picked up the local newspaper, ordered ham and eggs, and tried his best to concentrate on the real reason he came back to Tekamah.

He leafed through the pages of the *Tekamah Herald* to gather some sense of belonging to this town. Not many names seemed familiar in the headlines nor in the articles. He recognized an ad for Borge's Clothier. That must be Gomer's dad. Wonder if he knew all the shenanigans Gomer pulled when we were in school, and blamed most of it on me? Frank chuckled under his breath. Gomer always seemed to get away with his antics. Every prank was crazier than the next. If he had time, he would stop by to see if Gomer were still around.

He flipped through the pages toward the sports page in the back of the paper and almost breezed past the obituary column. The name jumped from the paper.

STANLEY MACKLIN WHEELER, AGE 75, TEKAMAH, PASSED AFTER A BRIEF ILLNESS. HE WAS PRECEDED IN DEATH BY HIS WIFE, IRMA MAE CONNORS WHEELER, AND TWO SONS, IRA MACKLIN, AND JAMES STANLEY. NO OTHER KNOWN SURVIVORS OR RELATIVES. A MEMORIAL SERVICE WILL BE HELD AT FAITH CHURCH, 235 13TH STREET, WEDNESDAY, OCTOBER 13, 1:00 P.M. VIEWING, TUESDAY, OCTOBER 12, 4:00-7:00 P.M.

Frank's heart felt crushed with a heaviness he couldn't explain, close to what he felt when his mother died.

Good ol' Mac. Mac was like a father to me for almost five years until he tried to sell me off for cheap labor. Frank shook his head to clear his thoughts. No. It was Irma Wheeler he hadn't trusted. Mac's missus never did like him. He wouldn't have put it past her to sell him off to a stranger for a few bucks. He felt a bitter distaste in his throat.

Guess I will never know. I would have never met my Anne had I not hopped the train to Wisconsin. It all worked out for the best and God had a plan –

or, has a plan, he corrected himself. There is always a plan, even if I cannot see it. That's what Anne would say, and I try to believe it, too. Can't always trust others or even my own judgment, but I can trust God who knows my tomorrows and what is best for me. 'Just believe.' That's what Mikie always said, and so did Anne.

Frank smiled. He missed Anne's innocent smile and her love for life. She had not written for some time, and he wondered how she was doing in college. He missed her words of encouragement. Anne was the one who urged him to come back to Tekamah, 'to straighten things out and give closure,' she told him. It took courage to make the trip, but now he was here. He would have to write and tell her. He felt guilty; he hadn't written for a long time. Told himself he had been too busy. Maybe a visit was in store for the future. Wonder if she still likes me? His heart thumped harder at the thought of a sweet reunion.

Mac deserved respects paid to him and Frank decided to attend the funeral. Besides, a few more days in town would give him a better perspective. He would visit some business places and see if anyone knew what happened to his siblings.

He decided better clothes than the jeans and t-shirts he brought were needed if he were to attend a funeral. The men's clothing store would be his first stop. After that, he would stop by the church. He hoped the same preacher who helped his sisters was still there. Perhaps he could get an address for them, or at least get some leads. He decided the police station would be another necessary stop. They may have some useful information, too.

Frank picked out a crisp, long-sleeved white shirt and a pair of dark trousers. His job on the mint farm and the grocer had done him well, plus Rev. Harley also compensated him for his services at the church. All in all, he had saved enough for this trip and a few extras. Besides, the funeral gave him a good excuse for some new clothes. A conservative gray and black striped tie completed the look. He tried on the trousers but was dismayed to find they were two inches too long. He could find nothing else he liked in his size.

"Do you do tailoring here?" he asked the clerk. "These pants need to be taken up."

"We send all our tailoring out, sir. It would take about a week to get them back. Is that all right?"

"No, I'm afraid not. I need these for a funeral in four days. Is there anyone local?"

The clerk thought a few minutes, tapping her pencil to her chin, looking somewhere under her eyelids. She seemed to be going through a mental checklist in her head, as she tilted it from side to side, pursing her lips. Then her eyes popped open as a big smile broke across her lips.

"I know just the one. She's an excellent seamstress, and she is quick," she paused, "but she lives several miles away."

"As long as it's within an hour, it's fine with me," Frank agreed.

She nodded, wrote the name and phone number on a scrap of paper, and handed it to Frank.

He thanked her and tucked the note in his pocket without reading it. He would get the trousers to this seamstress right after lunch. That would give her a few days to get it done.

Next stop: the church – where Mikie was killed.

Chapter 5 - Midnight Crisis

Dol twisted and turned to find a comfortable spot on the hard hospital bed. It felt as stark and cold as the sterile room she occupied. Her lower back ached in a hundred places at once. Wonder if this is how Ma felt when she was pregnant? If only she would have had help that awful night. If Pa could have only found someone to come help her in time. If only I could have helped her more..." Dolly's mind traveled back...

It was her mother's eighth birth and tenth pregnancy; two babies miscarried. Things had not gone well that day. Ma was having particular trouble; Dolly could tell even at age twelve by the way she massaged her back and held her stomach. She remembered helping with the laundry, then fixing lunch. Her mother's face was drawn and her breaths shallow as she clenched her teeth and bent over as far as her large stomach would allow, wrapping her arms around its base as if to hold it up. She had sat down at the kitchen table on a straight-backed wooden chair, and panted in uneven breaths.

"Dolly. Fix...the...san'...wiches. Call the kids...to

eat." Her voice came in short pants.

"Mama? You okay?" She had seen her mother with child before, but never like this.

"Just need...to lie down."

"Is the baby coming, Ma?"

"Help...me..." she gasped, "...to bed, Dolly." Her mother's face was pasty white. Her eyes reflected pain as her brow furrowed.

"Get...Pa. Quick."

***

Why can't I get it out of my mind? I wish I could have done more. Dol rubbed her back and then her belly as the restless child continued to tumble. She feared more spasms would come. Did Ma have this kind of pain too? She shook the thought and tried to turn on her side to alleviate the discomfort.

"Do you need anything before lights out, Mrs. Ryan?" asked the nurse at the door.

"No. I'm fine. Just an active baby, that's all. I know where the call light is if I need you," she reassured the nurse. "Thank you for all you've done. You've helped me have peace of mind tonight." That was all lies, she admitted to herself.

The nurse checked Dol's vitals one more time before leaving and then said goodnight, shutting off the overhead light.

Dol was restless; the baby didn't want to settle down no matter how much she massaged her stomach. She finally fell into a fitful sleep and dreamt again about the night her mother died.

***

Dolly had set the sandwiches on the table and settled her young brothers and sisters down to eat. She worried about her mother. Ma hadn't looked right. Such pain in her eyes. She hoped Ma could rest better lying down. She jumped as she heard a blood-wrenching scream. She ran to the bedroom filled with fear.

"Mama?"

"Get...Pa. Quick. Dolly. Need...him. Now."

Dolly's eyes grew wide at the sight of her mother, clutching her belly in pain, face grimaced and wet with sweat and tears. She ran to the field where Pa and her brother Guy were baling.

"Pa! Come quick. It's Ma. The baby's coming."

Pa ran to the house, knowing before he got there that his wife was in trouble. She wouldn't call him for help if she wasn't. She needed help fast. He ordered the kids outside.

"Grab your san'wich and git on the fence."

The children knew the rule. Anytime a baby was born or the kids were wanted out of the house, the fence out back became their sitting posts. "Ya'll take care of these little ones. Ah need to find someone to help yore Ma. Ah'll hurry to be right back," Pa had said.

But Pa didn't hurry fast enough. Dolly heard the screams time and time again. Her heart and gut wrenched, but she didn't know what to do. She wanted to help, but Pa said to sit tight. He returned empty-handed. The doctor was out of town; no midwife could be found. No neighbors were close enough to come.

Dolly watched in fear as Pa rushed into the house frantic with worry. Gracie hurried after him. Dolly ran in behind Gracie. That's when she saw all the blood. Ma was covered in it – the bed, the sheets, the floor. Ma screamed in agonizing pain. Pa pulled his hair and cursed.

Gracie's eyes grew large with fear and she began to scream.

"Git yore sista'. This is no place for her to be," Pa shouted at Dolly. Dolly stood frozen, her eyes glued on her mother. She looked like a wild animal caught in a trap writhing upon the bed.

"Git her out, I told ya."

She saw the despair in her father's eyes. He paced the floor and looked at her in desperation. Dolly turned away, unable to bear the sight she witnessed, the sounds she heard. Dolly snatched Gracie up in her arms and ran out the door.

Her heart beating out of control, Dolly awoke in the strange white room with the stab of her own sharp pains. Disoriented, she didn't know where she was.

A sharp cry escaped her lips as she turned in bed. Reaching down to put pressure on the pain in her groin, Dol was horrified. A wet stickiness soaked her gown. She pulled at the call light and slowly raised the covers, terrified. Sobs violently shook her body as her nightmare turned into reality. Bright red blood was everywhere – her gown, her sheets, her blankets. Dol's agonized scream alerted the nurses as another excruciating pain robbed her of breath. Her scream ended as she passed out into darkness.

Chapter 6 - Church Visit

Frank found the little church on the corner of 13th Street and Main. The name had been changed to Faith Church; additions had made the building look much different—much bigger. The street in front had been paved, the cobblestone gone.

He stopped outside the front doors and bowed his head. It had been eight years, but extreme sadness swept over his spirit as if it were yesterday. His mind heard the sickening crunch of a little boy's bones against the cobblestone and the screams of onlookers as they watched in terror.

Frank choked as he tried to breathe. The horror washed over him again as the scene vividly replayed. He watched himself unable to move, unable to help... or do anything. Mike gave his life for me. Pushed me out of the way and then got trampled and dragged to death.

Frank gathered his emotions, although his body was shaking, and entered the church. He walked the long carpeted aisle secured by rows of pews on either side toward the front. He knelt at the wooden rail altar and gazed at the simple empty cross which hung between the two stained-glass windows on the front wall.

"Why?" His shoulders shook as he silently sobbed and beat his chest with his hand.

"But I know where you are, dear brother." Frank let the tears stream down his face. "This was the big secret you wanted to tell me that Easter day. Now I know it too. Someday we'll be together again."

The minister approached from behind and laid his hand on Frank's shoulder.

"Something I can help you with, young man?"

Frank jumped, unaware someone had entered the room with him. His brain felt rattled. He fought to pull his thoughts together for the real reason he came.

"Oh. Ah...well. Ah, yes. Yes, you can." He swiped away at the tears which refused to stop.

The preacher motioned for him to have a seat on the front pew.

It took him a few moments before he could regain his composure. "My name... is Tim...Tim Larue. I used to live in Tekamah. My siblings.... and I...were separated after our parents left. I came back to search for them. I hope someone, like you, will remember something about them."

"About your parents?

"No," Frank responded, "my siblings. My brother and sisters."

"Are your parents still alive?"

"No. They are gone."

"Larue? Name sounds familiar." The preacher stroked his gray beard. A man came to mind, but he dismissed it. Decided against asking if he were one and the same. "Larue, you said?" He frowned.

"Yes, sir. Maybe you remember my brothers, Mike and Jesse? They lived with the Johnsons. I believe they attended this church."

The preacher nodded. "Oh, yes. They didn't have the boys too long, if I remember correctly."

Frank lowered his head. "That's right. Jesse died of the fever about a year after he moved there; he was always sickly. Mike had a terrible accident about a year later right in front of this very church." Frank couldn't stop the stream that spilled down his cheeks as he caught his breath.

Rev. Jorgens nodded and patted him on the shoulder. Frank became quiet as waves of emotion rolled over him.

"Seems... like...yesterday," he choked. He wiped his face. "I'm sorry..."

"You must have loved your brother very much."

"Not as much as he loved me, I fear. I owe him my life."

The minister nodded and waited a few minutes before he asked the next question. "And where did you end up, Tim? Don't remember ever seeing you in church."

"I went to live with the Wheeler's, Mac and Irma – I mean, Stanley and Irma Wheeler. They weren't church goers. He knew me as Frankie, my nickname. In fact, I still go by Frank."

"Ah, yes. Stanley Wheeler began to attend church here a couple years after his wife was put in the nursing home when she became feeble-minded. She passed last year. The farm got too much for him to take care of besides nursing her. Stanley passed a few days ago. Too bad you didn't get to see him. His funeral is this coming Wednesday."

"I saw his obituary in the morning paper. I plan to stay in town and pay my respects. He raised me for almost five years and was very influential in my life. I loved Mac like a father. The least I can do is say goodbye proper-like."

Frank stood to leave and then remembered why he came to see the preacher. "I almost forgot. My sisters – did they come to your house? Three of them. It would have been almost ten years ago. Were you here then?"

"Yes," the preacher stroked his beard again as he thought back. "Yes. Three young girls appeared out of nowhere. An older one, and two little ones."

"Dolly was twelve. Josie, six, and Gracie was four."

A light went on in the preacher's head. Larue. His sisters. Yes, I remember well. Old man Larue was their father – and this man's father. The town drunk.

"Do you know what happened to them, or where I can find them? I need to find them."

"They did come here, Tim. But I'm sorry. I do not know where they are now," the preacher said as he stood and looked past Frank towards the door.

Frank nodded with saddened eyes and headed out, head hung low.

"Come to church tomorrow, Tim. Ten o'clock. It may do you good."

Chapter 7 - False Alarm

When Dol awoke, she became aware of Ben's presence as he sat by her bedside. His head was bowed as he prayed quietly. Dol tried to sit up, suddenly alarmed.

"Did I...did I... lose...?" She couldn't bring herself to say it. She instinctively reached for her stomach.

Ben jumped from his seat to hold her in his arms. "No, no, Sweets. No, my darling," Ben soothed. "The doctor says you have nothing to worry about. There's just a very active boy inside kicking his way to get out."

"That's right, Mrs. Ryan," said the doctor as he entered the room. "Your placenta has been slightly ruptured, and you will need to be on bedrest for the final days of your pregnancy. But as active as this child is, that may not be long at all." He chuckled in an attempt to relieve her anxiety and the tension in the room.

"But...all the blood... too much...too soon." Dol couldn't make sense of it.

"Good thing you were here in the hospital, Mrs. Ryan, where people could respond within moment's notice, and where you could call for help in the middle of the night."

"He's right, Dol. I would say God had you right

where He wanted you. He helped you get the help you needed. The baby is safe; you are safe. Smile, Sweets. It's all good," Ben responded.

"I would like for you to stay in the hospital a couple more days, just to be sure," added the doctor.

Dol visibly relaxed as she laid her head back on the pillow. Then a frown creased her forehead, "But what about the girls? Who will tend to them? And what about you, Benny? The cooking? The cleaning? My sewing?"

"No worries, Sweets. Mama Vi won't mind having the girls stay for a couple days until you come home. You need the rest. You've been way too busy lately. When you get home, we'll hire some help, and as for your sewing, well, you can still do your hand work."

Dol was thankful for the lady they called Mama Vi. Violet Mae Hendricks was like a mother to her. Mrs. Hendricks took Dol in as a young apprentice and taught her the skill of a professional seamstress at a very young age. But Dol was not only an apprentice, Mama Vi treated her like a daughter.

Dol's face softened at Ben's tenderness and care. Her Benny always took care of things. She could count on his word. Relieved, she gave him a warm smile.

"I love you, Mr. Ryan." She paused as she

thought a moment. "By the way, did you say 'a very active boy?" her voice rose in excitement.

"Just hoping, Sweets," he grinned. "Just hoping."

Chapter 8 - Police Stop

Frank left the church confused. What did the preacher know that he wasn't telling? It bothered him. Was he hiding something? He would attend church tomorrow. Maybe he could get a better answer from the preacher after service.

Next stop:

the sheriff's office. The name on the desk looked familiar and so did the face – but Frank couldn't place him.

"Are you Sheriff Robert Stevens?"

"In the flesh. Something I can help you with?"

Once he heard the voice, he knew exactly how he knew him. Frank stepped back a couple steps to look him over. "Bobby Stevens?"

The sheriff chuckled and nodded, "Yeah...guess kids called me that back in the day. I grew up from those school days. You're Frankie, aren't you?" he grinned with recognition.

"Just Frank now. Surprised you remembered me. I wasn't there at school that long..."

"Long enough. You had the whole school talking after the stunt where you pulled Mr. Collins into the desk by his necktie and broke his nose. He was mighty mad at you; everyone was shocked how he kicked you out of class that day. You never did come back."

Frank nodded and chuckled. "Yep. That was quite a crazy mixed-up day. Hopped the train and left for good."

"I'm not here to talk about me, though, Bob. I'm here to find some information on my father or my brother. You may not remember, but maybe your father would remember something?"

"Like what?"

"Well, before I started to attend school, and before my younger brothers, Jesse and Mike, came to school..."

"Wait. Hold up. You say Jesse and Mike were your brothers? They didn't even have the same last name as you."

Frank chuckled. "That is because I told everyone my name was Frankie Wheeler. Pure lie. I didn't want anyone to know we were brothers. That's another story."

"Anyway, as I was saying, before we came to school, our Pa left us —seven of us, including me: four boys, three girls. Pa never came back, so we split apart. I asked for work at the Wheeler's farm; Mike and Jesse moved in with the Johnsons; Dolly and the girls went to the preacher's to see if he could help them find a place to live. Guy, the oldest, left to look for our Pa. I found Jesse and Mike at school again, but never did find where Guy, Dolly, or the girls ended up. I hoped by coming back to Tekamah, I could find someone who could shed some light on their whereabouts."

"You are right. I wouldn't know – before my time. But, my father was sheriff in town for the twenty years before I stepped into his shoes. He is retired now, but I can ask him. Stop by on Tuesday and you can talk to him."

Frank thanked him and left. He had a lot of time left in the day, so on impulse he dug the pencil-scribbled note from his jacket pocket and read the address.

Dolores Ryan, Seamstress
Arlington, NE. PH: 235-4433

He didn't remember where Arlington was located, but the clerk said it was a little town this side of Fremont – about thirty-five miles southwest. He figured he would get the trousers measured and then go back Monday to pick them up.

Frank found the small shop in the middle of a block of local businesses.

"Seen It – Sewn It Shoppe," said the sign on the door. Clever, thought Frank. The sign also said "Closed." Strange for a Saturday. On closer look, he saw another number.

Custom Tailoring
Special Orders: Call 235-2680

Frank found a phone booth, put in his dime, and dialed the number. A young lady answered.

Frank explained what he needed. She gave him directions to the house in the country north of Arlington. She explained the work would be done there. He would have to arrange a time to be measured and then pick them up the next day. Frank agreed to the plan and said he would be there first thing in the morning.

"I'm sorry, sir. You will have to wait until Monday morning to come," said the lady. "We are closed on weekends."

"That's fine," he replied. "I'll be there first thing Monday morning then. 9:00 a.m.?"

"9:00 a.m. will be just fine," she said.

Chapter 9 - The Call

"Who was that, Jenna?"

"A customer, Dol. Sounded like a young man. Wants his trousers hemmed for a funeral on Wednesday. He'll be here Monday morning."

Lizzie tugged on Jenna's arm. "Come on, Jenna. Let's play."

Jenna smiled at the little girl. "In a minute, sweetie. You all right, Dol? You look a little pale."

"Sweet Jenna, you are such a blessing. Whatever would I do without you? I hate this bedrest business, but it's what the doctor ordered. With you here to take care of the meals and the children, I can relax and not worry."

"You know it is my joy, my friend. I owe you a lot."

Dol laughed. "I thought it was the other way around."

Dol leaned her head back against the headrest of the chair and thought back. It was really Jenna who saved me.

***

Her whole being seemed to bubble with joy.

"Hi, I'm Jenna. You must be Dolly. Miss Smarkel said you'd be here today. I sleep on the bottom bunk, but you can have it if you want."

Dolly's eyes were focused on the nasty scar beside Jenna's right eye, but the girl was so bright and cheerful, it was easy to overlook.

"Ah, no – that's okay. I can sleep on top." Dolly looked around the room. Same as downstairs. Plain. Simple. The bunks were nice enough, but nothing fancy. Simple white blankets. Little two-drawer lamp stand between two sets of bunks. A throw rug covered the bare wood floors. One window with simple white curtains gave a little light.

"There aren't too many girls our age here," said Jenna. "So, would you be my friend?"

Dolly nodded and smiled. "Okay...I guess."

"If you need to know anything, just ask me. I'll help you. All the girls have chores to do. Most of the younger ones start by dusting or sweeping or helping with dishes. Some work in the kitchen and help cook or bake. I mend now, but I used to work in the kitchen."

"Where will they put me?" Dolly wanted to know.

"What can you do?"

"What do you mean?"

"Can you sew? Can you cook? Change diapers? What do you do best?"

"Oh. Well..." she paused to think. "I have always taken care of my little brothers and sisters, and that meant changing diapers, giving baths, making meals. I even helped with their reading and writing."

"Wow," Jenna grinned. "You have lots of skills. Which one do you like to do best?"

"I love to care for babies – guess that's my favorite thing. I love to rock them and sing to them and watch them fall asleep in my arms. They are so sweet and innocent. And, it's fun to teach them new things."

"Maybe Miss Smarkel will let you work in the nursery." Jenna said. "I will put in a good word for you. We better hurry to class. Can't be late. You heard what happens when we are late." She made her eyes large and scary-looking.

Jenna Martinez was the nicest girl Dolly ever met, and seemed so opposite of herself with her olive-skin and shiny black hair. She was curious about the scar, but Jenna acted like it wasn't there and never talked about it, so Dolly didn't ask.

She fell on her pillow that night with a multitude of emotions. She was thankful and happy for a new-found friend her age. She was sad to be away from her sisters. Encouraged and hopeful that she might get to care for babies in the nursery. Upset that she let her sisters down and broke her word to be with them. Fearful that Josie and Gracie would be given chores too hard to do. She worried about Gracie's weaknesses and frail body, but she was glad they were still all together in the same place, even though they were a floor apart. The jumbled thoughts finally retreated as her weary body gave in to sleep.

Jenna kept such a positive outlook on everything, never seemed depressed or hopeless, even though she hadn't been adopted. She seemed to bubble with enthusiasm and life. She turned her jobs into pleasure. Dolly determined to find out what kept her going.

A couple weeks passed as routines became the norm. Classes after breakfast, lunch, then chores, supper, then free time to do schoolwork before lights out. Dolly began to work in the nursery and toddlers' area, thanks to Jenna. She loved being with the babies.

"I will lavish you with hugs and kisses. I will treat you with the tender care of a mama you never had," she whispered in each baby's ear as she washed and cared for them. She loved to sing to the little ones while she rocked them to sleep.

Dolly was commended for her dedication to the children, and the leaders took note.

Jenna and Dolly talked often after the lights went

out, whispering back and forth from the top bunk to bottom bunk. They whispered at the wall so the others in the room could not hear.

"Jenna?" Dolly whispered one night.

"Yeah?"

"You asleep?"

"Not now," she giggled back, trying to be quiet.

"What happened to your parents?"

A long silence followed.

"Jenna? I'm sorry. You don't have to tell me. It's okay."

"No. I mean, yes. I want to tell you. I just get tearful sometimes when I think of them. I try my best to stay happy and thankful that I'm still alive. I lived when they died."

"Oh no. I'm so sorry."

"We were in a bad car wreck. Daddy lost control of the car. He was killed instantly. Mother was cut up so badly she bled to death before anyone could get there."

Another long silence. Dolly was sorry she had asked. This seemed painful for her friend, and she didn't mean to make her cry.

"It's okay," repeated Jenna. "They are in heaven now. I know it's true. They're watching over me, too, just like Father John said."

"Is that how you got that scar?"

"Yes. I was thrown through the window too, but

somehow I only got a bad gash beside my eye. I should have been blinded or worse, they told me. God saved me for a reason. I have to believe that, Dolly. So I try to be happy and thank Him every day."

It was Dolly's turn to be quiet. "Good night, Jenna. That reason may have been me. I'm glad you're my friend."

***

Dol was so thankful for Jenna. Mama Vi had graciously given her leave from work at her shop to come to Dol's rescue again. Jenna moved in with the Ryans during Dol's mandatory bedrest with this baby.

Jenna was indeed a gem. She was more than a friend; she was a sister.

Chapter 10 - A Look Within

Frank rose early Sunday morning, ate at Fanny's Café, and then headed toward 13th Street for the 10:00 a.m. service. He hoped to catch the preacher after service and have a few more words with him.

He settled into one of the back pews of Faith Church and watched as people arrived and took their customary seats. The recent renovation of the church gave it a modern look; the stained-glass windows were a nice touch. People greeted each other with smiles and hugs, in much the same tradition of his church.

As Frank scanned the parishioners, his eyes landed upon a middle-aged couple with two teenage girls. He wasn't sure at first, but the more he stared at the woman, he recognized her. Mrs. Johnson.

The same Mrs. Johnson who took his two brothers into their home. The Johnsons who let Jesse die when he was only six – the family who witnessed Mike's terrible, unthinkable accident being dragged to death by a wild, spooked horse.

An awful taste emerged in Frank's throat as bitterness crept up from somewhere deep within.

They let it happen, his heart accused. They

wanted me to come live with them – even after Mike died. His heart loathed being in the same room with them. He stared at them while they sang. How could they look so happy, knowing what they did?

Rev. Jorgens stood, greeted the people, and asked them to greet each other. A few turned to shake Frank's hand and welcome him to the service. He nodded, but said nothing. He couldn't pretend to be happy and refused to smile. He wanted to flee but forced himself to stay.

The preacher began, "This morning we will address a topic which many people struggle with - blame, unforgiveness, bitterness. It starts as a tiny seed, but once it takes root, it springs up as a mighty stronghold in your life. Bitterness can spoil everything you do for everything will be tainted with the ugly taste of something long past."

"Blame is a waste of time. No matter how much fault you find with another, and regardless of how much you blame them, it will not change the past or the present. But – it will change your future."

"Hebrews 12:15 says,
    "LOOKING DILIGENTLY LEST ANY MAN
    FAIL OF THE GRACE OF GOD; LEST ANY ROOT
    OF BITTERNESS SPRINGING UP TROUBLE YOU,
    AND THEREBY MANY BE DEFILED."

"Another way to say this is to watch for weeds of discontent. Just a few gone to seed can ruin a whole garden in no time. Do you feel angry or hateful toward the person who offended or hurt you?"

Frank put his head in his hands. Do I blame them? Yes. One hundred times yes – even if it was a long time ago. They should have protected my brothers but they did not. His heart roiled within his chest. He felt uncomfortable, exposed.

The minister continued. "Do you want to alienate yourself from them? If that is true, beware. You have the fruit of bitterness already taking hold of your spirit."

Frank squirmed and shifted his weight. He felt as nervous as he did the first time he attended church. His hands quivered; he shoved them into his pockets.

"Now, it is not wrong to feel hurt," Rev. Jorgens continued, "but how you deal with it makes all the difference in what happens in your life."

Frank wiped the sweat from his forehead and looked across the room at the Johnsons. They were listening intently, knowing nothing of what he felt. His own thoughts recoiled within, sending his mind down a wicked path of darkness. He wasn't sure how much of the sermon he missed, but he heard the next words.

"Forgiveness is the key. Matthew 6:14, 15 says:

"FOR IF YOU FORGIVE MEN THEIR TRESPASSES, YOUR HEAVENLY FATHER WILL ALSO FORGIVE YOU: BUT IF YE FORGIVE NOT MEN THEIR TRESPASSES, NEITHER WILL YOUR FATHER FORGIVE YOUR TREPASSES." 'SEVENTY TIMES SEVEN SAID JESUS.'"

"Forgiveness draws out the sting of the bee. It lets the past be past," the preacher continued.

Frank shook his head and again put his head in his hands. Forgive? How can I forgive? The turmoil in his heart battled against his thoughts. I thought this was past. Didn't I already take care of this hate and anger? His heart told him differently.

Frank looked at Mrs. Johnson again and was surprised to see her staring back at him with a large smile and a joyful look of recognition.

Frank quickly avoided her eyes, shook his head in disbelief and disgust, rose from his place on the back pew, and left.

The inner loathing surprised him as he hurriedly escaped the church. I refuse to listen to any more!

Chapter 11 - The Gold Pocket Watch

Frank's heart churned within. He kicked all the stones on the way to the car.

I am so angry. He thought he had overcome these emotions, but coming back to Tekamah tore off old scabs and reopened old wounds. He drummed the steering wheel as he drove, a myriad of thoughts whirling through his troubled brain.

He drove aimlessly with no sense of direction – out of town, past the Johnson estate, past Wheeler's farm, and found himself again on the dirt path of the old homestead. It was a good place to think.

He parked the car, got out, and surveyed the property again. He kicked at the dirt in disgust. How did we ever live in this dump?

Frank circled the old shack their family used to call home. Apparently no one lived in it since they left. The roof had begun to cave in, some of the dirt-encrusted windows were broken, and he couldn't remember if the shack had ever been painted. It was more in shambles than when he and his six siblings left ten years before, if that were possible. Inside, it looked much the same as when they left. Cupboards with open doors betrayed their barren contents; the stewpot still sat on the stove with unrecognizable contents.

Frank sat down on one of the wooden chairs at the small kitchen table where his younger brothers and sisters ate their last meal. He saw the young faces of Jesse and Mike, and an ache penetrated his heart. Each one looked at Guy as he announced his plan. Frank closed his eyes. The visual was real as his mind replayed the scenes.

He smelled the spicy aroma of Dolly's rabbit stew, and heard the thump as Pa knocked Guy to the floor. In his mind's eye, he saw Dolly's tears sneak down her freckled cheeks. He admired her brave front and wished for Guy's grown-up heroism. If only...

Frank banged his fist on the old table and tipped the chair over as he stood. That night changed our lives forever. He didn't bother to slam the door. Let the animals have the place.

The rickety old wooden fence lay in ruins rotting on the ground. He trudged the few yards to the barn – the barn that was once their haven.

Several rows of bales had been stacked high. In anger, he shoved them over revealing heaps of straw piled up on the floor. On top of the straw was a few dusty, crumpled, old blankets. Appeared as if someone made a makeshift bed to sleep on.

Dirty blankets, empty bottles and cans lay strewn about. He picked through the dishes and bottles, looking for some sort of clue. Anything. It didn't add up. Looked like someone had lived here, but who? A vagrant? Could Pa have come back and found us not here? Frank shuddered at the thought. Pa would have been furious. He would have become a lunatic.

Frank surveyed the other corner of the barn and saw a jacket hanging on one of the stall posts. He felt a shiver, though there was no breeze. It was Guy's too-small red and black plaid wool jacket – the one he wore the day they departed.

He picked it up and went through the pockets. Nothing. One of the sleeves was torn and bloody. Had Guy come back?

The noon sun peeked through a huge crack in the barn roof and bounced off a shiny orb on the floor. A glimmer of light shone in Frank's eye. He kicked away the straw. Underneath lay a golden pocket watch with a broken chain. He had seen a similar pocket watch many years before. Could it be the same one?

He picked it up and tried to open it, but it was broken. He turned it over and a chill went up his spine. On the back he read the engraved initials.

S.O.S.

Chapter 12 - The Preacher

Frank fumed in his hotel room that afternoon, disturbed by troublesome thoughts. Seeing the Johnsons again bothered him greatly. Brought a lot of hidden hate to the surface that he thought he had buried forever. The shack, the barn, and the third cross – what really happened? Had someone lived there? Did Guy come back – or Pa? It was a mystery. The preacher was hiding something. He knew something more about his sisters; he felt it. The conversation the day before ended abruptly and he felt pushed out the door. He had to ask why. There was still time for answers.

He knocked on the parsonage door. Frank shifted from foot to foot until the door opened.

The preacher looked surprised. "Frank, isn't it? Spoke to you yesterday at the church."

"May I come in, Rev. Jorgens? I have questions."

The preacher invited him in. "Millie, why don't you get us a plate of fresh cookies, and bring Frank some tea?"

"That's not necessary, preacher. Only need a few minutes to get to the bottom of things."

"I remember you were troubled yesterday when you left. Did you get the answers you needed this morning in the service? I saw you there."

Frank's eyes narrowed; his mouth tightened. "No. I did not get answers. I got more questions. That is why I am here. You weren't entirely straight with me yesterday, preacher," he said through clenched teeth.

Rev. Jorgens poured tea for both of them and sat down. His forehead wrinkled as he looked at Frank with a question.

"You know what I mean," Frank continued. "I asked you about my sisters. You weren't clear about their whereabouts."

"But I truly don't know where they are."

Millie Jorgens entered the room and took a seat by her husband. "We would have loved to keep them..." she started to say.

Jorgens gave her a 'don't-say-anything-more' look.

Frank looked past the preacher toward Mrs. Jorgens. "Tell me what you do know. I need to know."

Mrs. Jorgens ignored her husband's look and continued. "They were such sweet, innocent little girls, and the older one was so protective of them. She would have done anything for them."

"I told Charles I hated to see them go all the way to Lincoln. They would never see their brothers again. If they lived with a family here in town, at least they would be near their brothers."

"Lincoln?" Frank asked in surprise.

"Yes. We took them to the orphanage in Lincoln."

Frank sat back in his seat, stunned.

"So you see, we really don't know where they are. They probably have been adopted by now."

"How hard did you try? I mean, did you even try to find them a place to live?"

"We called the Wilmington's. They were young and had no children. They said they saw the need, but also said they were strapped financially. The cost of feeding three extra mouths wasn't feasible. The Browns thought it was a worthy cause, but felt their house was too small. We knew their five bedroom home was plenty big enough, but that was the reason they gave. I wasn't going to push. Of course, the Johnsons had already taken in your two brothers, giving them four children with their two girls. Most families had an excuse of some kind. I ran out of people in my church to ask. Finally, I called my friend, Judge Parson," explained Rev. Jorgens.

"The judge told me, 'The best thing for those girls is Overbrook Orphanage in Lincoln. They take in all kinds of abandoned and destitute children. It's a long drive from here, but the girls would be taken care of and the Home would be the best place to find a family to adopt them.' It was our last resort."

Frank's face fell. Millie Jorgens looked at him

with compassion. "We figured the Home could find a family to adopt them better than we could. I've always wanted children, and would have loved them with all my heart, but we are too old to raise little ones," she said.

"Gracie almost broke my heart the day we left them there. She ran to me, threw her arms around me, and hugged me tight. I didn't want to let her go, but the Administrator had already left the room with the other two girls. 'I'll miss you,' Gracie told me. I had to fight my tears away. We only had them four days, but they had already won a place in my heart."

"The drive home seemed long and dreary. I worried about the older girl. The little ones would be fine. They were sure to be adopted quickly. But Dolly? I was afraid of what would happen to her. The administrator told us they only kept children until the age of twelve. Dolly had told us she would be thirteen on her next birthday."

Frank was silent as the realization sunk in. He might never find his sisters. Thought he might as well ask about his father.

"And what do you know about LeRoy Larue?"

"The girls told us he was very drunk the night before they came to us. Left them and their brothers sitting out in the cold," said the preacher.

The preacher did not want to tell all he knew

about the town drunk. "Can't tell you much. You might check at the police station. Larue was known around the town."

Chapter 13 - The Seamstress

Monday morning found Dol in her sewing room. She sat in her rocker and soaked in the morning sunshine by her favorite south window. The leaves had begun to change color and she drank in the majestic hues of red, orange, and yellow. Her mums were in full bloom bustling with brilliant color. She loved this time of year. It was crisp, but not freezing cold. This was the time of year when weather could change in an instant, sending down sleet or an early snowfall.

It brought back memories. Her thoughts were many as she moved her needle in and out of the fabric. She wondered about this new baby coming, the past, and her own mother's difficulties with childbirth. She remembered the doctor's warning to stay on bedrest but figured sitting in her rocker to mend wouldn't hurt. Her daydreaming was broken by a knock on the door.

"Stay put, Dol. I'll get it," Jenna called from the other room.

Dol heard Jenna greet a man and invite him into the living room. She explained his trousers must be measured and pinned, and then they would be hemmed. He could pick them up in a couple of days.

"I need them by Wednesday morning, no later. Is that possible? I have a funeral to attend."

Lizzie skipped in beside her. "Who's this man?"

"This nice young man is here to get his trousers fixed, little miss."

Lizzie looked him over and smiled shyly at him.

Frank stared at the child. She reminded him of his baby sister, Gracie, with her blond curls, fair skin, and bright blue eyes. She certainly doesn't look like her mother, he thought as he noted Jenna's olive skin and straight black hair.

"Cute kid," Frank commented.

"Yes. She is adorable and I love her to death," she gave the little girl a squeeze. "Can you show the man the bathroom, Lizzie, so he can change his trousers?"

She nodded and grabbed Frank's hand to lead the way.

"When you are ready, I will measure them for length and pin them for Mrs. Ryan to hem. And yes, they can be ready by tomorrow."

"Oh." Frank raised his eyes, "I thought you were Mrs. Ryan."

Jenna blushed and smiled. "Oh no. I am just here helping her while she is on bedrest."

Frank came back with trouser dragging on the floor. Jenna told him to stand tall while she measured and pinned. She pulled her hair into a ponytail and knelt down to pin the hems.

Frank observed the young lady with new interest. He stood still and admired the features of this young lady kneeling at his feet. He noticed she wore no ring and looked to be close to his age. Her hair was as black as a raven's; her eyes sparkled when she spoke; her olive skin was polished and flawless – except for the scar beside her right eye. She had a rare beauty. Frank liked what he saw. Although she was business-like and professional, he was drawn to her gentle, quiet personality.

"There. Done. You can take them off now."

Frank looked at her with surprise and then broke into a large grin.

Jenna's face reddened a bright crimson when she realized how it sounded. "I mean, you can go to the bathroom and change. Be careful of the pins."

He gave her a wink and smiled all the way to the bathroom. He liked her already.

When Frank returned to the living room, Dolores Ryan was seated on the couch facing away from him.

He walked around the couch to meet her. His focus was drawn to the swollen abdomen, heavy with child; she looked quite uncomfortable.

"Hello. You must be Mrs. Ryan," Frank extended his hand without looking at her face. "I am so grateful you can fix my trousers so quickly. You see,

I have a funeral to attend Wednesday."

Dol reached her hand up towards Frank. A startling recognition hit them both as their eyes met.

Can it be? Dear God – can it really be? Frank searched her eyes for some sign of acknowledgment.

Dol looked at Frank with disbelief, yet hope. Silence filled the room. Neither spoke for several minutes. They searched each other's eyes. Frank couldn't find words. Dare he ask? His hand trembled as he clung to hers.

"I'm so sorry, Mrs. Ryan. You must excuse my rudeness." He let go of her hand. "It's just that..." he cleared his throat, "uh, well, uh...you look so much like someone I once knew. You caught me by surprise."

Dol grabbed his hand again, squeezed it tightly, and said in a husky voice close to a whisper, "Like your sister, Frankie?"

"Dolly?" Frank could not stop the tears. He recognized her voice. "Is it really you?"

Chapter 14 - Reunion

Tears of amazement and thanksgiving in her eyes, Dol pulled his hand toward her. Frank leaned down, hugged and kissed her.

They cried, embraced, and Dol began to giggle. "How can I ever thank God enough for bringing you back to me? You've grown so much. Look at you – a young, handsome man. You look so much like Pa. Where have you been? What have you been doing?"

Frank laughed at all her questions. He held up his hand motioning her to stop.

"When I saw the name Dolores Ryan, I didn't dream it could be you. I only knew you as Dolly. I asked the preacher in Tekamah where you and the girls were, but he said he didn't know. Yet, here you were all along, and not that far away."

"Well, Frank, the preacher didn't lie. He didn't know where we ended up. He and his wife took us in for a few days, but then..." her words faded and she closed her eyes.

Her voice brightened again. "Oh, we have so much to catch up on, my brother. Please. Please say you will stay a while and visit."

Frank settled into the over-stuffed chair while Dolly excused herself. He watched as she pushed her body up from the couch in obvious discomfort.

"Nature beckons," she apologized, patting her stomach. "I will be right back." She waddled out of the room.

Frank looked at his watch. It was close to noon. He didn't want to impose, but before he could protest, Jenna followed Dolly back into the room with a plate of sandwiches.

"You *will* stay for lunch, Frank. I won't take a no for an answer. Now tell me everything. I want to know it all. Where have you been? What have you been doing?"

Frank smiled at Jenna as she handed him a sandwich on a tray. She looked away, unnerved by his stare. Frank enjoyed seeing her olive skin glow as she blushed.

"Jenna's been my blessed angel," Dol said. "Don't know what I would have done without her. Jenna, this is my brother, Frank."

Dol settled back on the couch with her food. "What are you doing here in Arlington?"

"I came back to Tekamah to settle some scores in my life, Dolly. Most of all, I wanted to find you, the girls, and Guy. Maybe even Pa." He paused, unsure of how much he should disclose.

"I can't believe I found you. Guess fate is on my side." No. It wasn't fate, it was God, his heart convicted. "I mean, God must have directed my steps."

Dol's eyes twinkled in agreement.

"And I..." he hesitated. "I...found...Pa, too. I found him in the ground at the farm." He dug out the handwritten note and showed it to her. He watched her eyes grow big as Christmas dinner plates.

"So Pa is dead. Figured he would be by now, either from fighting or drinking," she said with no emotion. "LeRoy Larue. Found him. Buried him. SMW'," Dol read aloud. "What's it mean, Frank? Who's SMW?"

"Stanley Macklin Wheeler. Mac. The farmer I lived with. He's the only one I can think of. It looks like his handwriting. I was going to look him up to see what he knew about Pa. But then I read his obituary in the Tekamah newspaper. His funeral is Wednesday. I needed new pants, and they were too long, and — well, it looks like God led me right to you."

"What happened between Pa and Mr. Wheeler?"

"Don't know. Intend to see if anyone knows."

"Hmmm..." Dolly shook her head. "It's a mystery all right. What about Mike and Jesse? Last I knew Guy took them to the Johnsons in hopes they would take them in."

Frank frowned at the mention of the Johnson name and drew a deep breath. He frowned at his watch. His smile faded; his words were clipped. "It's getting late, Dolly, and it's a long story."

"I have time if you do," she patted her stomach again. "In fact, why don't you stay for supper? Then you can meet my Ben. We'll have the whole afternoon to visit."

Frank inwardly kicked himself. What am I doing? He changed his tone and smiled at her warmly. "Dolly, I would love to."

The rest of the afternoon flew as Frank shared his experiences while living with the Wheeler's and the friend he found in Mac.

"I found Jesse and Mike the following year at school. Jesse was so sick. He didn't make it long."

Dol saddened at the news. "He always had trouble breathing and the night in the barn couldn't have helped. What about Mike?" She observed Frank's face cloud over and a different person seemed to emerge. His demeanor changed; he stared at the floor. She watched his hands tighten into fists.

With a soft and husky voice, his voice caught. "Mike was killed. A terrible accident that shouldn't have happened. He was only eleven, Dol."

Dol put her hands to her mouth. "What?" she cried. "How?"

Frank retold the story of their brother's death.

Raw emotion surfaced again.

"Oh, Frank. That's horrible." She saw the anguish of his soul burdened with the weight of his brother's death and the knowledge that he couldn't prevent it. She watched his whole being recoil at the Johnsons for simply being there.

Frank grew quiet. Dolly dabbed her blue eyes as memories of their younger brother played in their minds.

"I saw them again, Dolly. Yesterday – at church."

"Who?"

"The Johnsons," Frank spat the name from his mouth. "They saw me too. Just seeing them makes fire in the pit of my belly."

"But why, Frank?"

"They should have done something–anything, Dolly, but they didn't. They let it happen. They let our brothers die."

Dolly felt his hurt and his anger. She was wrenched with grief.

Hesitant, Jenna broke the lingering silence. "May I take your tray, Frank?" she spoke gently.

Frank had forgotten she was in the room. She had heard his story too. He felt exposed. It was his turn to have the red face. He hadn't meant to reveal so much. Struggling to corral his emotions, he sat up straight, cleared his throat and became the old Frank again. He handed her the tray.

"Thank you, Jenna. And what about you, Dolly? You and the girls went to the preacher's, right? Where are Josie and Gracie now?"

The abrupt change in his behavior alarmed Dol. What had this boy been through?

Chapter 15 - Days Gone By

Dol thought back to that fateful day. "It was plain to see Pa wasn't coming back, Frank. He left in such a drunken stupor none of us knew what happened. It was no use waiting for him."

Frank nodded. It may have been ten years ago, but the memories were as vivid as yesterday. "There was no food and no heat, and we couldn't stay in the shack."

"There was only one answer. We had split up to survive and find our own way. Frank, it broke my heart."

"I know it did, Dol." Frank remembered the tears she fought to hide.

"Guy said he stayed up most of the night trying to think of a plan. If no one would take us, we would keep moving until someone did."

"Guy was supposed to look for Pa. If he found him, he said he would gather us all back together," recalled Frank. "Dol, have you heard anything from Guy?"

She shook her head. "No. Not a word. I was scared that day, but tried so hard to be brave. Guy was strong, the little ones dazed and so innocent.

They couldn't understand, but you – you, Frank, weren't bothered in the least. You had the look of a caged animal about to be set free."

He nodded and chuckled.

Dolly continued. "I had to support Guy. We girls watched Guy take the two younger boys and go one way while you went the other. Then we walked the few miles into town and arrived at the preacher's house right beside the church. With the girls hiding behind me, I approached the preacher's door and timidly knocked. My insides were full of butterflies. After a few minutes in the freezing cold, Rev. Charles Jorgens finally opened the door.

"'Well, well. What have we here? Do I know you girls?' he asked me. I was scared and embarrassed and ashamed. Told him he probably didn't because Ma and Pa never took us to church. I asked if he knew our pa."

"The preacher's eyebrows rose a quarter inch at the mention of our father, LeRoy Larue. He looked us girls over from top to bottom. Our faces were red and wind-whipped and our clothes tattered. Couldn't stop shivering and shaking in the cold wind."

"He brought us inside, and told his wife to get us some hot chocolate. He sat us down in the living room and asked us to tell him our story."

"We sat down on his couch, Josie and Gracie on

either side of me, clinging to my arms. I couldn't hold it in any longer. Everything within me flooded out like the gates of my soul had been opened. Seeing me cry made Josie and Gracie cry, too."

"He wanted to know who we were and said we looked real scared. That part was true. We were real scared. Asked if we were running away."

"Mrs. Jorgens set the hot chocolate on the coffee table and sat down beside me. She cloaked me in her arms and stroked my hair. She assured me we were safe now and whatever happened was over. She said we would be all right. Then I saw her give her husband an alarmed look. She wanted to know what happened and why we were there."

"So, in the next few hours, I described how we lived in fear of our pa. How I had to care for the children, cook, and clean. Between sobs and pauses, I spilled it all, past and present."

"Then I told them about the night before when Pa was drunk again. How he told us to sit on the fence and wait until he came back, and we all knew we would get a whipping if we disobeyed and got off the fence. How it got colder and colder. Remember how Gracie forgot her mittens?"

Frank nodded. "She always did."

"She was so cold, so I decided to lift her off the fence, and then talked Guy into doing something too. It was the first time any of us ever defied Pa. I was thankful and glad when Guy finally did something bold."

"That's when Guy thought about sleeping in the barn. We were lucky to pry the frozen door open," recalled Frank. "To me, it was all a big adventure – an opportunity to explore for myself and be on my own."

"For me, it was a great responsibility. I had the two little girls in my care. Mrs. Jorgens handed me a handkerchief, and agreed it had been a nasty night to be outside. The preacher was surprised to learn there were more children than just us three girls."

"Told him how the seven of us split up. Guy told us to come to the preacher's house because he would know what to do. He would know someone who could look after us."

"Preacher Jorgens let out a low whistle, shook his head, and then asked about you boys. Told him Guy took the two younger ones to the Johnsons and you went to Farmer Wheeler's. We didn't know what Guy was going to do."

"The preacher nodded toward his wife and said we could stay there for a few days until things were sorted out. Then she gave her husband a 'we-have-to-talk' look."

"She fed us a hot meal and gave us warm baths. She found us each a nightshirt. I felt relieved and finally safe. We had to share a bed, but that was okay. We would be all right. I only hoped you boys fared as well."

"Later that night, I could hear them talking from our bedroom. They thought we were asleep. Mrs. Jorgens asked her husband what they would do with us because they couldn't send us back home. She wanted to keep us, but it was not meant to be."

Chapter 16 - Dilemma

"Baby's sitting on my bladder, again," Dol complained, groaning as she struggled to rise to her feet. Frank helped her up, and she excused herself leaving Frank and Jenna alone.

"She is supposed to be on bedrest," Jenna said with a frown, "but she is a hard worker. Difficult to keep her down."

"That's my sister, she's always been like that. Do you stay with her all day?"

"And all night. I moved in after the doctor told her she needed bedrest for the remainder of her pregnancy."

Frank nodded. "She is very lucky to have you."

Dol rubbed her stomach as she came back into the living room. She eased herself into her chair and continued her story.

"Over the next couple days, I heard the reverend call several families in his small church. Finally, he sat us down for the announcement. I hoped he had found us a home."

***

"Girls, I think we've found a way to keep you all together."

"Our brothers too?" Josie's eyes lit up. "I miss Jesse already. He's my twin, you know, and even if he is a boy, I still miss him."

"I'm sorry, dear," Mrs. Jorgens interjected. "No, he meant just you girls."

"That's right. You three girls will get to stay together. We will leave tomorrow morning. There is a special place for children like you, and you can be with others your age. You will meet lots of new friends there."

The girls looked at each other, trying to decipher what was being said. It didn't make sense.

"You mean, like an orphanage?" Dolly asked.

"Yes, dear. The people there will help find good people to be your family."

Gracie looked at Dolly with fear in her eyes. "Do we have to go?"

Dolly hugged them both. "It will be okay," she tried to convince herself. "We will be fine. I will never leave you. We will always be together, I promise. Nothing is going to happen to my baby sisters. And, maybe someday, all of us, even our brothers, will come back together as a whole family again."

Rev. and Mrs. Jorgens exchanged doubtful looks, but they smiled and nodded.

They left for Overbrook Orphanage early the next morning for the long drive to Lincoln. As they pulled up to a huge four-story brick building with many windows, the girls saw children playing in the playground, all dressed alike. Most of them looked to be ten years old or under.

Inside the building, it was clean and spotless, not a speck of dust anywhere. Almost too clean, Dolly thought. It didn't look lived in. Rev. Jorgens met with Administrator Smarkel while Mrs. Jorgens sat in the waiting room with the three quivering girls.

"You will be fine," Mrs. Jorgens tried to calm the girls. "Did you see all the children outside? They all look happy."

Josie and Gracie sat with their little arms folded and legs dangling from the high couch. Big frightened eyes took in every detail of that strange place that didn't look like home. Gracie reached for Dolly's hand. "I'm scared, Dolly."

Dolly patted her hand and pulled her close. She was scared too. "I'll be right here with you, Gracie. Don't be afraid. I will never leave you. I promise."

Josie grabbed Gracie's other hand, squeezed it. "Me too, Gracie," she pinkie-promised.

The Reverend came out of the office with a smile and a nod. A thin, middle-aged lady followed him.

"Welcome to your new home, girls," she said in a high, squeaky voice. She tried to smile, but it came out crooked on one side, causing one side of her face to wrinkle up. A funny-looking wart wobbled on her chin when she talked.

Gracie squeezed Dolly's hand even tighter. Her eyes bugged at the sight of the old spinster who ran the home. Never married, Marva Smarkel looked much older than her early forties with her hair pulled into a bun perched high atop her head like a bird squatting in its nest.

"Stand, please," she ordered. She pushed up the wire-rimmed round glasses that balanced on her skinny nose and sized the girls up one by one.

"And how old are you?" she looked at Gracie.

Gracie held up four fingers.

"Hmmm. And you?" she asked Josie.

"Six," she answered in barely a whisper.

"And what about you, Miss?" she stared at Dolly, who stood almost as tall as the lady.

"I am twelve," Dolly said proudly, "soon to be thirteen."

"Hmmm," she said again as she pursed her lips. "I see. And when is your birthday?"

"I will be a teenager in two months."

"And you're excited about becoming a teenager?"

"Yes, ma'am." Dolly wondered about the question.

"Sisters, you say?"

They nodded. Gracie hid behind Dolly, her little body trembling.

"Good. Come this way, then."

The girls glanced at the Reverend, and then at Mrs. Jorgens for some sign of encouragement or hope or...or something.

Marva Smarkel nodded to the preacher and his wife as if that was enough for a goodbye, and trotted down a long, narrow hall with many doors on each side. The preacher and his wife turned and started to leave without saying goodbye. The girls stood frozen in place, staring first at the preacher, then his wife, and then at Miss Smarkel, not knowing what to do.

Gracie ran and gave Mrs. Jorgens a big hug. "I'll miss you," Gracie told her.

From somewhere down the hall, Miss Smarkel's squeaky voice called. "Are you coming, or not?"

The girls ran to catch up with her or be left behind, alone in her office.

***

"Frank, I didn't don't what was to become of us. I was determined to keep us together. I didn't know that was a promise I wouldn't be able to keep."

Lizzie ran into the room, interrupting her story. "Mama! Mama! Molly's choking." The little girl pulled on Dol's arm.

Dol gave Jenna a knowing look.

Jenna jumped up from the couch. "Sit tight, Dol.

I will see what's the matter." She hurried out of the room with Lizzie at her heels. "Did you give her something again, Lizzie?"

"Lizzie looks so much like Gracie did, Dol. Thought so the moment I saw her. I hope Molly's all right," Frank's eyes followed her all the way out of the room. "Jenna seems like a wonderful friend."

Dol laughed. "Lizzie likes to exaggerate – just like Gracie did. I'm sure everything is fine. Jenna will take care of it."

Chapter 17 - Life at the Orphanage

Dol continued her story. "We were brought to a large room with four bunk beds. There wasn't much space in the room. A small desk and chair separated the bunks with a throw rug on the wooden floor."

"Miss Smarkel told us we would share the room with three other girls temporarily. Two of us were to take top bunks, one the bottom. She told Gracie to take the bottom bunk since she was the youngest."

"The little girls thought it funny the way Miss Smarkel's wart bobbed up and down when she talked. They wanted to giggle, but were too scared, so they just stared at her wart while she gave instructions."

"Breakfast was 7:00 a.m. sharp. We were told anyone tardy would not eat until lunch. Lunch was at noon; supper at 5:30 p.m. We got three square meals a day, so no food was tolerated in dorm rooms. Anyone caught with food in their room was punished with one less meal the next day."

"Seems a little harsh," Frank thought out loud.

"You don't know the half of it. We had no other clothes except what we had on, but she told us uniforms would be provided."

"Both the girls were scared. I could tell by the way they squeezed my hands and wouldn't let go. I was nervous. Maybe we would have been better off finding our own place or staying at the shack."

"The Administrator trotted out of the room at such a brisk pace that day, I had to hurry to ask a question. When I did, she seemed perturbed," Dol remembered.

***

"Miss Smarkel?" Dolly asked in a quiet voice, but the lady hadn't heard, she was too far ahead. Dol ran to catch up to her. "Miss Smarkel?" she spoke a little louder.

The skinny lady came to an abrupt stop, almost causing Dolly to stumble into her.

"What *is* it, child?" She looked down her nose.

Dolly felt uncomfortable. She hadn't meant to make her mad. She cleared her throat, and asked timidly, "What did you mean by temporarily? I thought we were here to stay.'"

"This ward is for the younger girls, aged four to eight. The older girls, aged nine to twelve, live upstairs on the next floor. The room you will stay in tonight is for newcomers. Tonight, you will be allowed to stay with your sisters. Tomorrow, Miss Larue, you will move upstairs."

"But..."

"No buts. No ifs, no ands. That is our policy. Be thankful, young lady, that you can be with your sisters tonight."

Dolly thought Miss Smarkel sounded stern, but she could tell her eyes weren't harsh.

"Maybe you will meet some girls your own age on the upper floor. Most will be younger."

Dolly was afraid to ask what happened when she turned thirteen. That was only a couple months away.

As Dolly tucked the girls in their bunks that night, she told them. "Tomorrow, Miss Smarkel says I have to move upstairs with the older girls."

Gracie grabbed Dolly's arm. "No, Dolly. I'm scared without you here."

"Please, Dolly, you have to stay with us," Josie pleaded.

"I won't really be gone, girls. I'll just be upstairs, that's all. Josie, you have to be the big sister now. Look out for Gracie. You will have each other," Dolly tried to convince herself.

Josie nodded her head, but her blue eyes brimmed with tears. "...but you promised..." she cried.

Dolly's eyes were sad, but she forced a smile. "I know, sweetie, but it isn't my plan. I don't want to leave you. If it were up to me, I would stay right here and take care of you myself, but Miss Smarkel doesn't see it that way. She says it's policy. But I promise to see you every day at mealtime. Okay?"

Dolly's heart broke. Her sisters would be fine, she knew that. It was hard for her to stay strong and brave and not cry.

Morning came, and after breakfast Dolly was taken to the Jensen Wing on the third floor where the older girls lived. Most girls in this wing were nine or ten years old. Very few were eleven or twelve. Miss Smarkel was right, she was one of the older ones. She was introduced to the girl who would share her bunk, Jenna, one of the few twelve-year-olds. Without a smile, Miss Smarkel nodded at Jenna, and then briskly turned and scurried back down the hall, her bun bobbing all the way.

Chapter 18 - A Friend Indeed

Jenna came back downstairs with little fifteen-month-old Molly squirming in her arms. The baby reached toward her mother.

"Molly was fine," Jenna raised her eyebrows at Lizzie. Lizzie shrugged her shoulders, and skipped off to the other room.

"She took too big of drink from her bottle is all." She sat Molly on her mother's lap.

"Supper is in the oven, Dol. It will be ready when Ben gets home."

"Thank you Jenna, my dear friend."

Frank couldn't take his eyes off the dark-haired beauty. She noticed his stare and blushed deeply, enhancing her beauty even more. Dol noticed too, and smiled inside.

"Jenna's been my angel in more ways than one. Jenna was the first girl to greet me when I arrived at the Home. She helped me the most through the rough days. She was my first friend and bunkmate. Jenna also taught me to sew."

"Jenna would be a great catch for any guy, Frank. She has been waiting for the perfect man." Dol winked at her friend. "But I told her she will never find him – and yet, here you are," she chuckled.

"Dol," Jenna said, "You embarrass me."

"Me too," Frank confessed.

"Jenna was the one who challenged me to believe."

"How do you mean, Dolly?"

"Well," Dolly went back to her story, "I was concerned about Josie and Gracie, and I was worried about me. Something was going on, but I didn't know what. I confided in Jenna about everything."

Jenna chimed in. "There was a strict policy at Overbrook. Children could not stay past their twelfth birthday," she explained. If you weren't adopted by that age, they figured you had to learn a trade, go to work, or find a place on your own."

"October turned into November and my heart was troubled. Jenna's words stuck in my head. 'When you turn thirteen, you can't stay here anymore.' Where would I go? What would I do? I talked to Jenna many times at night," said Dol.

"We had a game we played after lights out. Sometimes we discussed serious things, other times we just talked. We whispered down the crack between the wall and our bunk so none of the other girls could hear..." Jenna laughed at the memory.

***

"Jenna?" Dolly whispered toward the wall to the bunk below, "Are you awake?"

"Yeah – I am now," Jenna giggled. It had turned into a fun joke.

"My birthday is next month."

"Oh, goody! We'll celebrate. Maybe Miss Smarkel will even get you a cupcake."

"That's not what I'm worried about, Jenna. I'm going to be thirteen." Dolly emphasized the number. "I'll be too old to stay here. What then?"

"Oh...yeah." Jenna whispered.

"When is your birthday, Jenna?"

"Not until next September. I won't be thirteen until next year."

They both quieted as the hall ward came to check the rooms. When they were sure they were alone in the dark again, Jenna whispered toward the wall.

"Don't worry. We'll figure something out."

***

"I lay wide awake on my bunk for a long time thinking that night. Jenna sewed and mended garments. She had a real skill. All I could do was care for the little ones, change dirty diapers, and bathe children. Thought maybe I could get a job as a nanny. I didn't want to go to the Industrial School for Girls, that was for sure."

"I tossed and turned in worry about my fate because Miss Smarkel had made it clear: children – boys or girls – had to leave Overbrook Orphanage once they turned thirteen. Most went to the Industrial School to learn a trade while they finished their schooling, or they chose to work. The path was clear: they left – one way or the other. Jenna always tried to assure me there was nothing to worry about."

"I told her to trust God because He was always there to help," added Jenna.

"Yes. She always said that. But how would I know? She always responded with, 'you'll know.'"

Jenna smiled at the remembrance and nodded.

"I didn't know what she meant and lay awake for hours staring at the ceiling. Where was God? And if he resided above, could He hear me? Tried to form questions to ask, but nothing sounded right. I was afraid to ask God about my concerns, worries, and fears. My problems seemed too small for a big God."

Frank nodded as he remembered his own journey. "It was much the same for me, Dol."

"I finally dared to wake up Jenna to ask. I whispered through the crack between the wall and the bunk below."

"Jenna?" All was quiet.

"Jenna," I whispered louder. "You awake?" I

even wiggled in the bunk to make the whole bed shake.

"I remember that night, Dol," Jenna laughed. "I am now," she mimicked a sleepy voice. She giggled. "Then she asked me a question I will never forget. 'Can you teach me to sew?' she asked."

"In the next few weeks, Jenna worked with me on the simple running stitch to baste two pieces of material together, then taught me the blind hem stitch. She brought me pieces of material to practice on so I could sew hem stitches close to invisible. Once I was proficient on those, she taught me the more difficult stitches, like the overcast and whip stitch."

"I practiced on the small garments Jenna brought. It took several times of ripping out hems and starting over before I really got the hang of it. Discovered it was something I really enjoyed. Soon, Jenna brought me some of the boys' shirts and pants and other jumpers to be hemmed. Since I worked in the nursery, I could sit in the rocker by the fourth floor window and hem while the babies napped. That is how I learned to sew, and it has taken me far. I have always been thankful for my friend." She smiled at Jenna, who stood to her feet.

"I'll get supper on the table, Dol, and feed the girls so you can visit with your brother. Ben will be home any minute."

Frank waited until she was out of the room before he spoke. "So she lives with you?"

"She still lives in Fremont with Mama Vi, but during my time of bedrest with this pregnancy, she agreed to come live here with us. She has been a huge blessing."

"I saw how you looked at her, Frank," Dol gave him a motherly stare.

"Jenna is a beauty all right," Frank admitted.

"You seem quite taken with her. "What about you? Do you have a girl?"

Frank reddened. "That noticeable, huh? It was my Anne who guided me on the path to belief. In fact, it was Anne who talked me into coming back to Nebraska to bring closure to the events of my past–to make peace with myself. It took me a year and a half to make this trip. I guess I was afraid of what or who I'd find. But now, I am thankful I came back."

"Because now you have found me, Frank. We are family. Think of what you would have missed had you not come. Please, tell me all about Anne."

"I haven't heard from her in a while—too busy at church and at work. Plan to make a surprise visit to her soon." Frank shared how he met Anne and how it was mostly a long distance relationship. "We don't see each other often. She's at college now."

Dol saw Ben's car pull into the drive. "Oh, good.

Ben is home!"

Ben rushed through the door, concern written all over his face. "Dol? You all right?"

"Benny, we're in here," she called from the living room.

"I saw the strange car in the drive – it's too late for customers, and it didn't look like the doctor's car. I thought... I was afraid you..." He looked at Frank with suspicion.

Dolly held her stomach and giggled. "Benny. Benny. You're such a worrier. But you're my sweet worrier and I love you for it.

"We have a special guest for supper tonight. Meet my younger brother, Frank – all the way from Wisconsin. He is the one I told you about – the one who went to live with the farmer."

Chapter 19 - Won on a Bet

"You, know, I won your sister on a bet," Ben joked and winked at Dol as he stuffed a forkful of potatoes into his mouth.

"Oh, Benny. Will you never let that go?" Dol gave him an exasperated look, but a silly school-girl grin crossed her lips.

"Ben and I met in high school when I lived and worked with Mama Vi at her dress shop in Fremont. She insisted I attend school and not slack on my education; she wanted a smart seamstress."

"I tried for months to get her attention," said Ben, "and she treated me like dirt."

Dol pretended to scowl. "I never treated you like dirt, Mr. Ryan. My eye was on you too."

"It was only the first or second week of school when I bumped into Ben as he came around the corner. We were in many of the same classes."

"Bumped? You ran straight into my arms, Dolly, my girl," Ben teased.

"Books flew all over the hallway. I didn't know whether to laugh or cry or run away. All Benny did was laugh at me. I was so mad at him." Dol gave Ben a fake glare.

"I tried to help you pick them up," Ben tried to frown and sound wounded. "I knew right away that I had found the pearl of great price – my gem." He patted her hand.

"I was so mad, I stormed away and wouldn't speak to him for weeks," Dol grinned.

"She wouldn't give me the time of day and avoided me at every turn. Julius bet me I would never get her to like me. In fact, he said he would win her over before I did and take her away. The game was on."

Frank was intrigued as Dolly and Ben told their story. Love was evident in their faces as they recalled their past.

"So, what changed your heart?" Frank pointed the question toward Dolly. "How did he get you to change your mind? How did Ben win the bet?"

"Benny never gave up. I ignored him, avoided him, and shunned him for almost two years, but he was always there every time I turned around. Always kind, but not mushy, pushy, or forward. Julius tried to get me to date him, but he wasn't my type and I wasn't interested. Little by little, my reserves gave way and I realized I really liked Benny. We dated for the last year of school and married the summer after we both graduated."

"Lizzie came along the next summer."

"I am happy for you Dolly." Frank rose from his

chair and looked at his watch. He saw the tiredness in her eyes, even though her face was enveloped in gladness. "You must be spent. I must get back to Tekamah."

"I hate for you to leave, Frank. I just found you."

Frank laughed. "Well, I know where you live now, Sis. Besides, I have to come back tomorrow to pick up my trousers anyway."

"You're right, of course. It is getting late. Why don't you come for supper again tomorrow night?" Her eyes lit up, "In fact, why don't you bring your luggage and stay at our house the rest of your stay in the area? It would give us both time to catch up," Dollie thought out loud. She saw Ben give her a sideways glance with a small frown.

"Dol, you promised me you would get your rest. You know what the doctor said," cautioned Ben.

"I will – I will. But it's been ten years since I have seen Frank. We have lots of catching up to do," she pleaded with her eyes. Ben nodded with a scowl. He knew she would have her way and he loved her too much to argue.

"Well, if you are sure it's no bother," Frank replied ignoring Ben's look. "I really do want to hear about your journey, and find out more what happened to Gracie and Josie. Where did you say they are?"

Ben stood to his feet and put his hand on Frank's

shoulder. "Tomorrow, Frank," he said with sternness in his voice. "Got to get my girls to bed."

Ben swooped Lizzie up in his arms making her giggle. "Tell your Uncle Frank goodbye, Lizzie."

Chapter 20 - Searching for Clues

Frank had all day Tuesday to sniff around town before he headed to Dol's. He hoped to dig up clues to Guy's whereabouts. Maybe he would find more answers concerning his pa as well. He checked out of the hotel and stopped by the police station right after breakfast.

The retired Sheriff Stevens sat behind the old oak desk as if he owned it, feet propped high, leaning back in the chair with his fingers interlaced behind his head.

He acknowledged Frank as he entered the room, removed his feet from the desk, and sat up. He gave Frank a wide grin and held out his hand.

"Timothy Larue," Frank said as he pumped the older man's hand, "but your son knew me as Frankie Wheeler." He chuckled at the inquisitive look he received. "Tried to run from my past back then. LeRoy Larue was my father. Do you remember him?"

"Bob filled me in on part of your story. I wouldn't have pictured a clean-cut guy like you as the son of that old drunken bum – excuse me for being brash – but you do look like him. Your old man was in the slammer every other weekend back in those days.

Only way to dry him out was to throw him in jail for a couple days."

Scenes from the past started to make sense to Frank – the nights Pa failed to come home and the lack of money for food and supplies, the days he came home so drunk he either flew into a rage and trashed the shack or beat up Mama or Guy. Those rough years suddenly became very clear. He and his siblings were aware of Pa's drinking problem, but they didn't understand consequences back then. All they knew was Pa was often too drunk to care and there was nothing to eat.

"Sometimes a young husky boy about 14 or 15 came and dragged him from the bar or picked him up from jail," continued the older man.

Frank pulled a chair up to the desk. "That would have been my older brother, Guy. I know it's a long time ago, but do you remember seeing my Pa or Guy in October of 1936?"

Sheriff Stevens scratched his head as if itching out a long hidden memory.

"That is a long time ago, kid. Like I said, every other weekend or pay day, LeRoy Larue was in town drinking at the bar or fighting with the men in the bar. Gambling. Carousing. Brawling. Drinking. Sorry, son, but that was your pa."

The old sheriff's eyes lit up. "Now that I think of it, there was a pretty bad brawl back then. Larue was always getting into fights, but with one man in particular because of his gambling. They were both arrested. Both looked roughed up. Must have gotten an earlier start on their drinking binge and gotten into a fight at the bar. Yep. He was a mess, all right. Spent the night here in jail. Released them both the next morning, if I recall. He didn't come home?"

"No, sir, he did not. In fact, I'm still looking for him," Frank lied. "Looking for my brother Guy, too. Do you remember if Guy came to look for him the next day?"

"No. Don't remember seeing him. Sorry I can't be of more help, son. You might check McGraff's Bar, or some of the other bars in neighboring towns. He visited them all." The sheriff's head bobbled as he nodded and shook his head at the same time. "In fact, can't remember seeing Larue around here for some time now."

Frank thought in silence a few moments. "You said he often fought with another man. Maybe he would know what become of my father. What was his name?"

The old sheriff laughed. "Those two were sparring buddies, I swear. Seemed to fight over everything – their drink, their women, their cards. Yeah, I remember him. His name is Sy Simmons."

Frank left the sheriff's office with a knot in his

stomach. Simmons knew Pa?

He headed down the street to McGraff's Bar. It made him uneasy to step into those surroundings, knowing it was the very place Pa used to frequent and squander the family's money. The more he found out, the sicker his stomach felt. He took a seat at the bar and waited for the bartender to finish an order. When the bartender looked at Frank, his mouth dropped open.

"Well, I'll be. If I didn't know better, I'd swear good ol' LeRoy was back from the grave."

Frank's head reared back with question in his eyes, his brow furrowed.

The bartender realized his forwardness and apologized. "Sorry," his face reddened, "ya just really look like LeRoy Larue – a guy who used to hang around these here parts a lot in his day. Hasn't been here for several years now. Figured he moved, or died, or something."

Or something, thought Frank. "Actually, that is why I am here. I am LeRoy's son."

It was the bartender's turn to look surprised.

"I'm trying to find what became of my father. He abandoned me and my brothers and sisters long ago. He left in a rage. Thought he came to town to drink, like usual, but he never came back. Didn't know if he got himself killed, or if he just left.

Thought maybe someone might remember where he went. Was he here?"

The bartender gave a belly laugh. "Hah! He was always here. But, give me an approximate date."

"October – mid October, 1936."

"Well," he scratched his head, "gonna say he was prob'ly here. But then he may've gone to one of them other bars around the area. LeRoy liked 'em all: Uehling, Blair, Logan, Herman, Craig...."

Frank shook his head. "Thanks, anyway."

All the smaller towns were within a thirty mile radius. He hoped to glean some useful information from at least one of them. A couple taverns were on the way back to Dolly's home outside Arlington. The first few he visited gave no information on his Pa's whereabouts, but they did remember LeRoy Larue.

"A scrapper," some called him. "Held his liquor," said others, "but made him crazy."

No one remembered anyone coming to get him, or Pa fighting with a man named Simmons – until he hit Shaker's Bar & Grill in Blair.

Chapter 21 - Blair, NE

Frank drove to the spot in the road called Blair, Nebraska. It sat twenty miles south of Tekamah, over half-way to Arlington. The tavern was easy to find in the tiny town with only one gas station and not much else.

Frank walked into the tavern, sat down at the bar, and asked for the owner. A gruff man with unshaven beard appeared. He wiped his hands on the dirty apron he wore, and quizzed Frank with his eyes.

"Doing double duty," he explained. "Bartender quit. What do you want?"

Frank explained his crusade to find his father and brother.

The owner gave Frank another look-over and let out a low whistle. "You're the picture of your old man —those fiery eyes and red hair. Ain't seen him in a while now. Wondered what happened to him. But yah, he came in here real often. Liked to play cards and gamble and flirt with Lily Sue."

Frank frowned at the news, but it gave him hope.

"Not a good gambler either, if I 'member right. Lost lots of money and made lots of enemies at that table right over there," he pointed to the one in the corner. "Got into some nasty fights, too."

"He and one other guy in particular were always at each other's throats."

"Let me guess," said Frank. "My pa owed the other guy money."

"...or over a woman," chuckled the man.

"What was the man's name?" He guessed he already knew the answer.

"Simmons. Sy Simmons. Used to come across the river to gamble over here. Think he lives somewhere around Modamin – in Iowa."

Frank cleared his throat and nodded.

"Would you have an address? Or a phone number?"

"Simmons keeps an open tab here at the bar – pays up when he gets the money. That's why he was always scrappin' with people who owed him money, like your pa." He dug in the cash drawer. "Well, here's his phone number anyway."

Frank stuffed the number in his pocket. He had to talk to his sister about Simmons and see what she knew. For now, he had to hurry back to Tekamah; Mac's viewing started at 4:00 p.m. Tuesday afternoon.

He filed in with a few others and waited in line to view Mac's body in the casket. For some odd reason, his nerves were jittery with an unexplainable sorrow in the pit of his stomach.

As he approached the casket, he was taken back. Mac appeared so old. Only five years had passed since he left, but it looked as if those five years had taken its toll on this man he had learned to love. An unexpected lump caught in Frank's throat as he recalled the experiences he had at Mac's farm and the many times Mac spared him from a tongue-lashing or a beating that his missus wanted to dole out.

Frank bowed his head and silently gave thanks for the old man who took him in as a youngster. Mac was a good man. His face looked beaten and weather-worn like a piece of old leather, yet he had a peace on his face.

Goodbye, Mac. I will never forget all you did for me. I hope to see you in heaven someday.

Rev. Jorgens waited until Frank finished paying respects and then motioned for him to step into a side room.

"After you left the other day, I began to think. You said Mac knew you as Frank, is that right?"

"Yes," answered Frank.

"There were a few papers left in Mr. Wheeler's belongings and a couple of letters. The nurse found a single envelope laying on the desk by his bed with the name, 'FRANK.' You must be the Frank it was intended for. I brought it with me."

The preacher dug the envelope from his suitcoat pocket and handed it to him.

Curious. I left nothing behind, and Mac had nothing to give. Frank took the envelope and tucked it in his pocket.

Once in his car, he couldn't wait to dig it out. Slipped his finger underneath the seal and opened it. The letter inside had Mac's handwriting.

Stunned as he read, his mind churned. Another drunken brawl gone wrong? Did Simmons come back to finish the job? The pocket watch he found proved Simmons was at the barn. Mac saw him too. Would he ever know?

Chapter 22 - Moving In

Frank was glad Dol invited him to stay with them. Finally, real family. He arrived at the Ryan's country home early that afternoon. He wanted to share with her what he found out about their Pa and wanted to know what she knew about Simmons.

If Simmons' story was true – that he was really the biological father of Guy, Dolly and Frank, and that their mother left him when Frank was a baby – then maybe Dolly remembered him.

He was anxious to see Jenna again. Thoughts of Anne were pushed behind as the vision of this black-haired, dark skinned beauty invaded his mind.

He pulled up the long narrow drive lined with small bushes here and there on either side. Ben Ryan had inherited a modest two-story, four-bedroom home in the countryside north of Arlington, Nebraska. As a lawyer, Ben was able to provide nicely for his family. Frank was happy for his sister. She deserved the best, and it appeared she got the best in Ben.

A wide grin appeared across Frank's face as

Jenna met him at the door with a smile. She seemed just as glad to see him.

"Dol is resting, and the girls are napping," she half-whispered with a finger to her lips. "Come. I will show you where to put your things."

Jenna led him up the stairs to a bedroom across the hall from where she slept. A little thrill crawled up Frank's spine to realize he would be so close to her. Lizzie and Molly shared a room down the hall. Ben and Dol had moved to the first floor bedroom so Dol could stay on bedrest during her pregnancy.

Frank unpacked his few clothes and started to go downstairs when Lizzie saw him.

"Mr. Frank! You're here." She squealed and tugged at his hand to pull him toward her room. "Come see."

He marveled how much the little girl looked like Gracie. Same blond curls and blue eyes. Same fair skin. Even had a dimple in the exact same spot. He felt like his eyes were playing tricks.

She showed him her dolls, her toys, her room. Baby Molly played in her crib until she saw Frank come closer. She pulled herself up to the rail and held her arms up.

"She wants you to pick her up," said Lizzie as she pointed toward Molly.

Frank wasn't sure what to do. He had never held a child in his arms before.

The baby started to fuss, and Lizzie stood there staring at him with her hands on her hips until he took the hint and lifted Mollie from the crib. He was surprised how light she felt. She immediately cuddled in his arms and laid her head on his shoulder. It gave him a warm feeling to have the child take to him so quickly. He patted her back as he took her downstairs into the kitchen with Lizzie close behind.

Jenna gazed out the frilly-curtained window as she peeled potatoes. To Frank she seemed the natural homemaker. She cooked, she sewed, she knew how to take care of children. Seemed she could do everything.

"What have we here?" Jenna smiled seeing the threesome.

"I found some new girlfriends," Frank teased which made Lizzie giggle.

"Can I help?" Lizzie asked. "Mama lets me help."

Jenna patted the little girl's bottom. "Not now, little one. You scoot." She looked into Frank's eyes, and then looked quickly away. "In fact, you all scoot. Out of here," her voice was playful. "I need to finish supper."

Frank pretended to look rejected, but couldn't help but grin.

"Come visit, Frank," he heard Dol call from the living room. "We have plenty of time before Ben gets home and before supper's ready. Jenna will take care of things out there."

"Yes, Ma'am!" He winked at Jenna on his way out making her blush again. He smiled—and so did she. It made him feel good.

Chapter 23 - Josie and Gracie

Frank set Molly on the floor to play and then settled on the couch. Lizzie jumped up beside him and snuggled against his arm. Frank curled Lizzie's blond curls around his finger.

"Can't get over how much she reminds me of Gracie. Same curls, same blue eyes."

"Just like our Mama," Dol commented.

"Tell me, Dol. What happened to our baby sisters?"

Dolly repositioned herself in her favorite over-stuffed chair, put her feet up, and closed her eyes tight. Her forehead wrinkled at the memory.

"I let them down, Frank. I told them I would always be there for them, but I couldn't keep my word. That will haunt me to the end of my days. Thanksgiving 1936 was the last time I talked to them."

"Almost ten years ago? That was right after we all separated, then."

Dol nodded. "Yes. Gracie was so excited to tell me about the couple they had met. She told me stories of being adopted. I wasn't sure whether to believe her or not. You remember how Gracie loved to play make believe, so I almost dismissed her babble – until I saw the black sedan pull away from the orphanage one cold day. They were in it." Dol's mouth tightened.

Frank folded his arms and frowned. "A black sedan?"

She nodded. "I was real worried and talked to Jenna about it. She always told me to believe for the best and trust in God, and I tried."

"Thanksgiving was only a few days away and one of the rare times when all the children were gathered together for a grand meal."

"Josie and Gracie ran toward me and Jenna as we came downstairs to the dining hall. Gracie threw her arms around my waist and almost knocked both of us to the floor," Dol laughed as she remembered the day...

***

"I miss you soooo much."

Dolly returned the hug and then hugged Josie. "I've missed you both too," her face showed her pleasure at seeing them again, "and I'm so sorry we can't see each other every day. I thought there would be a way."

Gracie couldn't contain her excitement. "Guess what?" She grinned and giggled as she grabbed Dolly's hand.

"What, sweet pea?" Dolly sat on her haunches

and bent her knees to look Gracie in the face. "What has you in a dither?"

Gracie put her hands on Dolly's cheeks to focus her face to her sister's. "We're getting a new mama and papa!"

Dolly almost toppled off balance at the news. "What?" She raised her eyebrows. She looked at Josie with an 'is-it-true?' look but, Josie just shrugged her shoulders and refused to look at her sister.

"Well? Is it true, Josie? Or is Gracie just making this up?"

"I...I...think so. I'm not sure," Josie hedged.

"It's true, Dolly," Gracie defended with her little hands on her hips. "And we're all going. They said. And they're getting us puppies and dolls and a pink room and everything."

"Gracie, you don't know that," Josie scolded.

"Gracie...." Dolly started to reprimand her for telling stories.

"Do too know. That's what she said."

Her voice betrayed the worry she felt. "Who said?" She shot Jenna a look of alarm.

"The pretty lady," Gracie defended with innocence of a four-year-old. "The lady with the blond hair. They came to find us. She was real pretty and smelled real good and told me I was pretty too and said that I looked just like her when she was a little girl," she bubbled without taking a breath.

"What was her name?"

"Joan. And the real tall man's name was John." "They're really nice and they look really rich. The lady had on a pretty gold necklace and a fur coat."

"What did they say?" Dolly was getting more concerned by the minute.

"I overheard the man say he wanted to keep the sisters together. What's that mean, Dolly?" said Josie.

Gracie made her voice sound high to mimic Miss Smarkel. "She said 'Good job, girls. You made me proud. You made a very good impression on your new mother and father.' They'll be here by Christmas to get us." Gracie giggled. "I'm so excited!"

"Did they talk to you, too, Dolly? Will you get to come with us? I want you to come too," Josie sounded as if she would cry.

Dolly's stomach knotted up into a tight ball. No, they hadn't talked to her. In fact, she hadn't seen the couple or been told anything about anyone. Maybe the girls just got things mixed up. Maybe they just misunderstood. She couldn't let them see her worry. Dolly looked at her little sisters and forced a big smile.

"Everything will work out just fine. You wait and

see," she said with another quick hug.

"We'd better hurry to the dinner table. This is a very special meal and we don't want to be late," reminded Jenna. Throughout the meal, Dolly was unusually quiet.

"It will be okay, Dol," whispered Jenna. "It will all work out, like you said."

"I know. I hope it's all their made-up story, Jenna, but I also know they both want a real mama and papa to care for them. I just can't get their words out of my head."

Dol pushed her turkey and dressing around on her plate, hardly eating a bite. Her gut hurt too much.

After the meal, the girls spent the afternoon together. Jenna stayed with them.

"I helped put all the silverware on the table for the Thanksgiving meal, Dolly. Did it look good?" Gracie beamed.

"I helped make the special name cards and placemats for the meal," added Josie.

"They were wonderful, girls," Dolly tried to be cheerful. "Tell me about your classes."

"We're in different rooms in the morning," Josie explained, "but in the afternoon we get to play together. I met Janis and Kathy and Penny. They are all my age. Janis helps me with my reading, and our teacher is nice, too."

"What about you, little one?" Dolly stroked Gracie's curls.

"I have new friends too," she bubbled. "Lissy, Sylvie, and Mary, but I like Mary best. Lissy still sucks her thumb," said Gracie.

Dolly felt a sadness inside. They hadn't missed her near as much as she had missed them. At least they were both doing well, she told herself, and seem to be adjusting to this new life.

"Tell me about the lady, Gracie."

"You should have seen her, Dolly. She had a sparkly gold cross on her necklace, and a fur coat that was so soft," Gracie went on. "She had blond hair and blue eyes just like mine."

"What did you think, Josie?" Dol asked.

Josie shrugged her shoulders and refused to look Dolly in the eye.

"There must be something about them you can tell me. What about the man?"

"I didn't look at them much, but the man was real tall. He had to stoop when he went through the door. They told us they didn't have any children of their own. The lady said we were making her dream of little girls come true."

Dolly tried to smile, but her gut hurt even worse. She didn't want anyone to take her sisters away, but what could she do if they did? Would she ever see them again? She hoped it was all the dream of two orphaned girls.

"Almost time to go," one of the workers announced, coming into the room where they sat.

"Already?" Gracie frowned.

Josie ran over to Dolly and gave her a long hug. "Promise me you won't leave us, Dolly. Promise me you'll come too if we have to go."

Dolly's heart tugged hard. She sucked in her tears and struggled to keep strong. They must not see her cry. "In only a couple of weeks we will be together again, on Christmas Day. Maybe you will get to set the table again, Gracie," Dolly tweaked her nose.

"I'm sorry we can't have the same meal times. I tried real hard to get work as a server so we could see each other in the lunch line, but it wasn't possible. They needed me in the nursery."

"That's okay, Dolly. Christmas isn't that far away," Josie said. She tried to sound cheerful, but her eyes showed sadness, and the smile would not come. "Maybe we can be together for your birthday, too," Josie hoped.

Her thirteenth birthday. Dolly nodded and blew them kisses as they were guided to their rooms, but her mind went dark. And then what would she do? She knew what happened to those who turned thirteen.

C.A. Simonson

Chapter 24 - The Black Sedan

"You said the girls rode off in a black sedan. Whose black sedan?" Frank wanted to know.

"That's the part I don't know–the part that will always bother me. Afraid I'll never know."

"The week before Christmas, snowflakes had begun to fall on the Nebraska flat lands. The ground was covered with sparkling white. I remember that day well. As I gazed out the window from the fourth floor nursery, I marveled at the glistening trees waving their white-gloved fingers. Across the meadow from the orphanage it appeared as if diamonds covered the landscape as the sun's rays bounced off the snow. It looked so clean and fresh."

"I sat in awe and thanked God because I knew and believed the idea of learning to sew came from above. Maybe it would prove to be something more someday."

"I was caught up in my thoughts and the beauty outside, when my attention was diverted to a shiny, black sedan which had pulled up in front of the building. A man in a gray suit got out and entered the building. The woman remained in the car. Curious, I kept watch because I had never seen them before."

"Then Josie and Gracie came out of the building with Miss Smarkel and the man. They had on new winter coats and boots and walked toward the car. I jumped from my chair to get a closer look. Alarm started to rise deep inside of me. The lady got out of the car to greet them. Gracie ran to her. The lady extended her arms and welcomed Gracie."

"What did Gracie do?"

"Gracie wrapped her arms around the lady and gave her a long hug. I began to believe there was something to Gracie's story."

"Did the girls seem frightened?" Frank asked.

"Gracie looked happy – full of smiles. She jumped up and down when the lady handed her a pretty frilly-dressed doll with golden curls. She hugged the lady again and then hopped into the back seat of the car. The lady turned toward Josie with another doll in hand."

"What did Josie do? You said she didn't seem as excited as Gracie about the couple."

"Josie lagged behind. Miss Smarkel placed her hands on Josie's shoulders and seemed to coax her forward to the car."

Frank noticed Dol's teeth clench as she relived the scene.

"When Josie reached the car, she stood still and lifeless, although the lady tried to hug her. The man bent toward her and whispered in her ear. Josie shook her head. It appeared she was arguing with him. She pointed back toward the building."

"Do you think Josie saw you in the window?"

"No, I don't think so. I sat like a stone statue— unable to think, speak, or act. I wanted to run and rescue them, but didn't dare leave the babies alone. I could only watch the scene unfold and pray it wasn't what I feared. I felt helpless, Frank."

"Did Josie look afraid of them?"

"No. She looked defiant, Frank. She looked like someone swatted a mad hornet within her. The lady tried to give Josie the doll again, but she batted it away, knocking it from the lady's hand to the ground. Josie ran back toward the building. She was crying. I thought I saw her mouth my name. Did I only imagine she called for me?"

Dolly paused and shook her head as she recalled that awful day. Frank sat on the edge of the couch intently listening. He felt his own nerves tighten as he imagined his little sisters being taken away.

"Miss Smarkel caught Josie by the arm and forcefully guided her back to the black sedan," Dol continued. "My heart pounded as the man picked Josie up and placed her forcefully in the back seat. He closed the door and then the couple got into the front seat. Josie pressed her sad face against the back window of the car as they drove away. She was crying."

"Frank, my heart felt torn from my chest. I couldn't breathe. My body felt as if it were dead weight. I couldn't move or cry out. I didn't know where they were taking them and tried to convince myself they were going for a simple ride. Maybe the couple was taking them for a holiday meal. I heard of other children being taken to people's homes for the holidays or for a special meal. I couldn't believe they would be going away forever."

Frank felt the anger in his own heart begin to rise. "What did you do, Dol?"

"I panicked. I began to believe Gracie's story was true. The more I thought about it, the angrier I became. Why wasn't I informed? Why didn't the couple ask about me? Why didn't Miss Smarkel say something? Why? Angry and confused, I determined to have my say with Miss Smarkel. It wasn't right, and I was going to let her know how I felt."

Chapter 25 –
Meeting with the Administrator

Dol's neck turned red and her eyes held fury as she told the girls' story. Frank realized old wounds had been ripped open and it brought pain for her to retell it. He felt helpless.

"Dol, if this is too much..." his face showed concern, "you don't have to continue. I don't want you to overdo it."

"No. No, it's all right, Frank. You need to know what happened and then maybe you can help me know what to do. It stirs my fury, that's all." Dol readjusted her weight and rubbed her stomach to ease the child into another position. She took a few deep breaths as she replayed the scene in her mind.

"I fumed the rest of the day thinking about Josie and Gracie. I formed a plan to see Miss Smarkel. I had to get to the bottom of it."

"Once my shift was over, I worked up the courage to approach the Administrator. I remember how scared I was. I sucked in a huge breath. With knees knocking, I rapped on her office door...

***

"Come," the high-pitched voice called from behind the door.

Dolly opened the heavy oak door, and saw Miss Smarkel crouched behind her desk, head bent over paperwork, hair piled high with the customary bun on top. She removed the round, wire-framed spectacles from low on her pointed nose, and looked up in surprise.

"Yes, Miss Larue?" her voice squeaked.

Dolly took another deep breath and determined not back out or back down. "I want... I mean, I...I...have to ask you a question," Dolly stuttered, half in fear, half in doubt.

Miss Smarkel poked the pencil into her bun and looked Dolly square in the eyes. "Very well. I have to ask you a question, too. Please sit down."

It took Dolly off guard. She took a few wobbly steps backwards before she caught her balance. She sat warily on the couch.

"You will be thirteen at the end of this month, am I correct?"'

"Ah...yes ma'am. December 28, but I..."

"That is correct, Miss Larue. And how old will you be?"

Dolly was flustered and confused. Miss Smarkel knew the date of her birthday, and she knew very well she would turn thirteen. Why was she asking these questions? "I will be thirteen, ma'am."

"You answered correctly again. And have you been told what happens to the children at the home who become teenagers?" She removed the pencil from her bun and tapped it on the desk as Dolly remained silent and nodded her head.

"You understand the policy," she said. "It was explained when you arrived. Twelve-year-olds have three choices: they can go to the Industrial School and learn a trade; they can stay here, provided they have a viable way to give back to the home; or, they can leave and find their own way – unless they are adopted into a family, of course." She had a tight-lipped half smile like that wasn't going to happen. "Have you thought about your options?'"

Dolly stumbled on her words, disturbed by this odd line of questioning. "Maybe there's some family in town who would hire me as a nanny? Or somewhere that would let me take care of babies?" Dolly toed the carpet, nervous in the pit of her stomach. What exactly did she mean by a 'viable way to give back'?

"Well, now, Miss Larue. That is very commendable. You have done a wonderful job in the nursery. The children love you, and it is evident. You are an excellent caregiver and viable teacher."

Dolly's eyes brightened with understanding.

"I will put your name out in the community for nanny jobs if that is what you desire. But if you want to stay here at the orphanage, you would have to agree to work in the nursery and teach the toddlers. This would be without pay, of course. Your room and board would be your pay."

Dolly's mind was rattled. She knew this day was coming, but now it was only a month away. Her mind traveled in a hundred ways all at once. She loved the children, and that would be a way to stay in a familiar place and to be with her friend another year.

A thought popped into her brain; she wasn't sure where it came from, but decided to take a chance. Maybe it was only a pipedream, but what would it hurt to ask?

"What's on your mind, Miss Larue? You look deep in thought."

Dolly looked up at the Administrator and took a big breath. "What if I could mend and sew clothes for the children?"

Miss Smarkel's high-pitched voice rose even higher. "You can sew?" Her interest was piqued.

"Well, I know how to hem."

"I've noticed the superior work on many of the uniforms. I thought that was Jenna's handiwork. You are telling me it's your work?"

"Yes, ma'am. Jenna's been teaching me."

"Hmmmmm," she scribbled some notes on her paper. "Very interesting," her squeaky voice cooed.

Dolly was suddenly worried for her friend. Did she say too much? "Jenna won't get in trouble, will she?"

"Jenna should not have given you her work and pretend it was hers. I will deal with her later."

Knowing Jenna would be 'dealt with later' scared her. Miss Smarkel could be a frightening lady. Dolly's nerves tensed.

"It is good you learned to sew, Miss Larue. I will thank Jenna. It appears she has been a very good teacher. The home always needs good seamstresses to sew and mend the children's uniforms." She wrote a few more notes on her paper.

"You have three weeks to make up your mind. Whatever you decide, we will help make the transition, whether you decide to stay here and work, go to the Industrial School for Girls, or leave to find a job."

Dolly stood to her feet and tried to search for a hole to crawl into. She didn't know what else to say. She felt as if she'd been punished – or was about to be.

"You can go back to your room now. Good talk."

Dolly turned to leave with head hung low. Her whole body felt like a deflated balloon. She walked slowly toward the door and then suddenly remembered why she had come in the first place. The image of Josie and Gracie being driven away in a black sedan flashed through her mind and made her angry again. With a fresh boldness, she spun around to face the spinster.

"Wait," she squinted her eyes at Miss Smarkel, "What about my sisters?"

Miss Smarkel had already returned to her paperwork. "Yes? What about them?" she asked without emotion.

"You *know* what about them," Dolly dared to raise her voice in defense. "I saw you march them out the door to a black car this very afternoon."

Marva Smarkel raised her eyebrows in mild shock. She laid her pencil down and maintained her staunch composure. She stared at Dolly but did not answer.

Dolly dared to approach her desk. "Were they were just going for a visit? Did that couple take them for a meal? Please. Tell me. I need to know."

The administrator bit her lip, and pushed the glasses higher on her nose. She tapped her fingers on the desk as she thought out her answer. She spoke low and stern. "Close the door, Miss Larue," she said very slowly, "and sit. We need to talk."

Scared, but mad, Dolly backed up a few steps and again took a seat on the couch.

In a matter-of-fact voice without feeling, Miss Smarkel explained how a young couple came to look for two little girls. They loved Josie and Gracie, and the girls had been adopted by this fine family. The paperwork had been completed and all legalities taken care of. "The girls left this very afternoon to go live with their new parents," she said without smiling.

"Without even saying goodbye?" Dol was dumbfounded and stared straight ahead as if in a dream. This couldn't be happening. She had sworn to never let it happen. She couldn't believe her ears, but now she knew Gracie had been telling the truth. She heard herself somewhere in the distance, "Who are they?"

"Sorry, Miss Larue. I am not allowed to let you know that information. Don't worry, the girls are with a fine, well-to-do family. They will provide sufficiently and treat them kindly."

"Do they live in Lincoln?"

"Privileged information. Sorry."

Dolly's brain felt muddled. Her heart was being ripped apart. She raised her shoulders, sat up straight, and dared to speak up again. "Josie said they didn't want to split up the sisters."

Miss Smarkel pushed her chair back, stuck her pencil back in her bun, stood up, and stared at the bravery of this girl who dared to speak her mind. She raised her eyebrows. "She heard us say that?"

Dolly nodded, her lips pursed.

"Thought we were out of earshot of the girls.

That is unfortunate," Dolly heard her say under her breath.

"Josie thought all three of us were going to be together again."

Dolly noticed the Administrator's tight face soften. She came around the desk and sat down beside Dolly. Marva Smarkel put her arm around her. An unusually compassionate touch from such a tough lady, it made her suspicious. She felt herself grow even more tense.

"That explains why Josie was so insistent to get to you, I guess. She thought you were being left behind...and she was right. I am sorry, Dolly. The couple only wanted younger girls, like your sisters. They did not know about you, the older sister.'"

And you never told them about me, cither, Dolly fumed inside. Now she not only felt deflated, she felt defeated – and rejected. Left behind to find her own way. Dolly's eyes teared, up but she choked the flood away. This woman would not see her break down and cry.

"I saw Josie kick and cry as she tried to get away. She tried to run back to the building. But you – *you* and the man made her get in the car. She didn't want to go. She called my name," Dolly's voice quivered.

"Josie wanted to come get you, Dolly. And she wanted to tell you goodbye. I couldn't allow it. I am sorry."

Dolly couldn't hold it in any longer. The burden was too great. The flood broke loose and she bawled. Miss Smarkel sniffled a few times herself. She gave Dolly a slight squeeze on her shoulder and dug out her handkerchief.

"The girls will be fine. I promise."

"But they are my sisters, and I promised to take care of them. I said I would never leave them."

"You don't have to worry anymore. They will be well taken care of."

"Will I ever see them again?" Dolly wiped her eyes and dared to look at the woman.

"No," she shook her head. "I am afraid not." Her tone was soft; her eyes showed empathy as Marva Smarkel thought of her own lost siblings never found.

"Will you ever tell me?" Dolly's eyes pleaded as she asked.

Marva Smarkel shook herself and became business-like and cold again. She removed her hand from Dolly's shoulder and stood.

Her tone was flat. "No." Her voice hardened with finality and a 'never-ask-me-again' sound.

"What will become of me?" The teary-eyed Dolly also stood.

"We have already discussed that, young lady. Go back to your room now, and let me know when you've made a decision."

Marva Smarkel turned away from Dolly. She didn't want the girl to see the mist in her eyes. But her voice had betrayed her.

***

Dol wiped the tears from her eyes as she relived the story. Frank knew her wounded heart had been reopened by telling the story of losing her two baby sisters. It wounded her just as much as losing his younger brothers hurt him.

Lizzie hopped into the living room. "Jenna says supper's ready. Come on," she tugged at Frank's hand to pull him up. "I want you to sit by me."

Chapter 26 - Dolly's Fate

Dolly waddled to the table as Jenna put the finishing touches on the meal.

"I asked Jenna to join us tonight. You don't mind, do you, Frank? Jenna, there's an empty seat beside Frank."

"Aww, I wanted to sit beside Mr. Frank," scowled Lizzie.

"You get to sit on the other side, Missy," smiled Dol.

"You're not playing matchmaker, are you Sweets?" chuckled Ben.

She gave him a glaring smile. "Now Mr. Ryan, have I ever?"

Jenna wondered too; she had always joined them for dinner. The extra attention made her self-conscious. She was glad her scar was on the opposite side of her face.

Frank enjoyed Jenna's presence beside him. Made him feel...complete. It seemed right somehow.

Between bites and news of Ben's day, the dinner hour flew.

"You were about to tell me what happened on your thirteenth birthday."

She tilted her head back to recall a long ago past…

"I didn't know what was to become of me, Frank. I was scared. I worked hard and continued to improve my hand stitching. Jenna taught me the most difficult stitches."

"She was a natural," admired Jenna, "and a quick learner."

"Miss Smarkel often bragged that not one hint of thread could be found on my perfectly blind-stitched hems. She seemed pleased with my work. I didn't know she had been making other plans for me already."

"A few days before Christmas, I found a note in my room to report to the Administrator. I bit my nails as I walked to her office on the first floor. That day her door was open, inviting, and festive-looking with Christmas decorations. I stood at her door, fearful to enter unannounced."

"She wanted your decision?" Frank asked.

"That's what I thought. My thirteenth birthday was less than a week away. I still hadn't decided what to do. Didn't want to go to the Industrial School, and sure didn't know anyone in Lincoln. I leaned toward staying at the orphanage as long as they'd let me, or at least until Jenna had to leave."

"I wasn't sure whether to enter or not. Inside, a huge box wrapped in Christmas paper sat on the coffee table in front of the couch. I looked first at her, and then the box and asked with my eyes if I should come in.

"Her squeaky voice welcomed me in. She sounded so joyful, it made me afraid – especially when she told me it was Christmas and I was almost a teenager."

"What did you do? What was in the package?" Frank asked.

"I wasn't sure what was happening. Should I sit? Stand? I fumbled with my hands and shifted my feet. Expected to be asked if I had made my decision. My time was up for the orphanage unless I offered my time and work for room and board. Should I stay at the home? Should I go to school and learn a trade? Should I venture out on my own? Frank, I was so confused."

"Was there any possibility of adoption?"

"It wasn't likely anyone would adopt me at age thirteen. Eleven? Twelve, maybe. But at thirteen, I was old enough to work. If I stayed and kept my job in the nursery, I would be with Jenna and the little ones I had grown to love. At least that would better than being turned out into the street. Didn't know anyone outside the orphanage, and certainly didn't know where to go. The thoughts overran my mind like a steaming freight train as I silently stood before Miss Smarkel's desk."

"She told me, 'Dolly, don't just stand there, girl. Come. Sit down. I have a gift for you.' Marva Smarkel almost bounced toward the wrapped present, giddy with glee, and unbelievably friendly."

"I perched on the edge of the couch, suspicious of this new side of the straight-faced administrator. I wasn't sure what to make of it all. Why would anyone give me a gift, and who would give it? None of the other children received special gifts."

"She told me to open it, so I unwrapped and opened the box. My heart leapt when I saw what was inside."

"Wait until you hear this, Frank. This is priceless," Ben's eyes twinkled as he watched his wife retell the story.

Dolly looked at him and grinned. She took a bite of her chicken and slowly chewed, enjoying the suspense she was creating.

"Well? What was in it, Dol?"

She motioned with her hand to wait until she finished her bite. "A sewing machine. A real sewing machine. I couldn't believe it. Did I dare believe what I hoped? Was it really for me? Started to say I didn't even know how to sew. Miss Smarkel giggled a little and told me I could learn. Her excitement matched mine as she watched me admire the machine."

"She said I had shown increased achievement and had a great aptitude for learning. My hemming and mending skills had proven impeccable in only two short months. 'Someday,' she said, 'you will become a magnificent master seamstress.'"

"And you have proved it true," Jenna glowed.

"She asked if I was willing to learn to use it. Felt like I was in a dream, Frank. The slick black machine felt so smooth, so shiny and new. I nodded that I would learn, but couldn't find my voice."

"Then she said there was only one small condition."

"Of course there was a condition," grinned Jenna. "I lived there long enough to know that Miss Smarkel *always* had a condition."

Dol nodded. "I kept my mouth shut and backed away from the gift to sit on the couch. I folded my hands in my lap and waited for her verdict."

"She noted my apprehension and told me not to worry. She thought I would love her idea. Said the home really needed me and didn't want to lose me. Commended me for taking care of the children and said I was one of the best preschool teachers they had ever seen. Thanked me for being a big help with mending and hemming uniforms and was thankful Jenna taught me."

At the mention of her name, Frank jerked self-consciously, and turned toward Jenna. She reddened and lowered her eyes.

Frank breathed in her flowery scent as she sat next to him at the table. It was heavenly. He felt pleasure in the closeness of her body, yet guilt. What about Anne? He pushed the niggly thought from his mind. Anne hasn't written me in months.

"So, what was her one condition?" Frank asked as he tried to keep his mind on the conversation.

"She said they desperately needed someone to help make uniforms for the children. She wanted me to learn to sew professionally – to learn the trade of a seamstress."

"By that time I was shaking. I asked how? Jenna had already taught me everything she knew. We didn't have machines at the home that I knew of."

"We had sewing machines, Dol. We hadn't gotten that far in your sewing lessons, yet. Besides, I was still taking lessons myself," explained Jenna.

"Violet Mae Hendricks," Ben interrupted. "Our beloved Mama Vi was the key to the plan."

"Gramma Vi," corrected Lizzie with her mouth full.

"Yes, Gramma Vi," Dol lovingly nodded at Lizzie. "The girls think of her like their own Grandmother Ryan. Well, Miss Smarkel told me Violet Mae Hendricks, a professional seamstress, lived in a town north of Lincoln. She made most of the uniforms for the home and needed help. She would train me if I would become her apprentice."

"It sounded too good to be true. When I asked if I would still live there at the orphanage, she said no. That was the one condition. I would have to agree to go live with Mrs. Hendricks. Mrs. Hendricks was a widow who worked from her home in Fremont. She would give me room, board, and training in trade for work." Dol raised her shoulders and took in a deep breath.

"Sounds like a good deal," Frank commented.

"I still had almost a week to give it some thought, but I didn't have to think about it or even talk it over with Jenna. I was willing, and wanted to learn how to sew with a machine. Thought maybe someday I would have a sewing shop of my own." She paused and smiled at Ben.

"Guess that part of your dream came true," Ben winked at her with pride in his voice.

"Because you believed in me – and my dream," she beamed at her husband.

"She left me that day with a Merry Christmas and Happy Birthday. Miss Smarkel notified Mrs. Hendricks the first of the year to help with the transition. I moved in right after the New Year and brought my sewing machine with me. That is how I ended up living with Mama Vi."

"Mrs. Hendricks was much younger than I thought she would be for a widow. Smartly dressed, well groomed, and very business-like. Intelligent, too. She was an industrious woman with an amazing skill of sewing. She started her own sewing shop from her home after her husband was killed in the war. Soon she had a thriving business, not only in Fremont, but also with work from the orphanage in Lincoln. I called it fate."

"I called it faith. Faith in a God who would work all things for the good of those who loved him," added Jenna. "It was perfect for Dol, and it turned out to be for me as well."

"Jenna had no family either, so when she turned thirteen the next year, I asked Mama Vi if Jenna could come live with us too. She agreed whole heartedly. Two professional seamstresses added to her shop only made her business boom.

"After I married Ben, Jenna kept right on working for Mrs. Hendricks, and eventually came to work part-time for me."

"And I am so glad I did," responded Jenna. "You saved me, Dol. Where else could I have gone?"

Chapter 27 - Who is Sy Simmons?

"I'm glad things worked out for you, Dol. Still, it is discouraging not to know where Josie and Gracie are. Maybe someday, we'll find them."

"Yes. I hope so," Dol said.

"Jenna – wonderful supper," Frank put his hand on her shoulder as he pushed his chair back from the table. "You're going to make someone a great wife someday."

"And I think I know the perfect man," Dol teased and winked at her.

"Dol. Quit," Jenna blushed as she rose from the table. Her sparkling black eyes smiled at Frank, and he felt his heart skip a beat.

Jenna offered to clean up the table and then bring dessert to them in the other room. Ben said he would help. Dol and Frank retired to the living room and Frank pulled the gold watch from his pocket. "I have something to show you, Dol."

She took it from his hand to inspect it.

"It was laying on the floor in our barn, broken. Found it today. Looked like there had been some sort of scuffle there. In fact, looked like someone had been living in the barn for a while."

She squinted to read the back engraving: "SOS?

What does it mean?"

"I have my suspicions." He narrowed his eyes; his mouth became tight as he spoke. "Dol, what do you know about a man named Mr. Simmons?

"Don't know anyone by that name. What about him?"

Frank told her the story about Simmons coming to visit him when he lived with Mac, and said he was his biological father. "Said Ma divorced him when I was a baby. Said you and Guy were his kids, too. He knew you by name. The day he came for me, I hopped a train and ran away. Did he ever come to the farm when we were kids?"

"Not that I know of. If it's true what he told you, then you would have only been two years old when Ma left him, and I would have been four. My memory would be vague, and you wouldn't remember at all. Guy would have been almost seven, so if anyone would remember Simmons, it would be him."

At the mention of Guy's name, silence stretched between them as they sipped their coffees and their thoughts trailed to the past. Both wondered where their older brother ended up, or if he were still alive.

"Did Simmons ever come to look for you, Dol?"

"Don't think so. He wouldn't have known I was at the orphanage, and they would have been too protective anyway. Think he gave up trying to find you?"

"Yeah. He didn't know where I went. No one did. Didn't bother telling anyone. I believe that is his gold watch. I remember it clearly. I may have only met him once, but he made a show of dangling that watch like a charm."

"Mac thought Pa was living in the barn. Who knows? Maybe Pa found Simmons living there. Anyway, according to Mac's letter, he found Pa and Simmons in a huge fight. Had to tear them apart before they killed each another. Said he chased Simmons away. Here. I brought the letter with me."

Dolly sat back in her chair and massaged her belly as the baby gave another sharp kick. It took her breath away. She changed position, and frowned as she read.

Dear Frank –

Don't know if you'll ever get this letter. Felt real bad 'bout how we all parted ways. Never did know where you went. If I did, woulda sent it to you.

Gotta tell you 'bout your pa – your real pa.

Saw you out of the corner of my eye coming up the road the day Simmons came for you. Hated for you to go with him. We waited and waited, but you never came.

He was madder than a wet skunk. Said I broke the agreement. Bound and determined to find you. Simmons thought you went to the farm to hide there. Don't know how he knew where it was.

Worried about you and followed. Found him fighting your pa over you. Simmons swore he would take you away too.

Your pa tore into him like a mad wolverine. Looked like they were going to rip each other apart. Broke 'em up.

Told Simmons to leave and don't come back. He fumed, but left, far as I know. Your pa was real drunk. Went back to check on him after a couple days. Found your pa by the barn door face down in the dirt with a bloody shirt, deader than a possum. Looked like he dragged himself to the door.

Don't know what happened, but thought he should be buried proper-like. Found him. Buried him. Told no one.

That's the least I could do, Frankie.

Sorry.

Mac.

"So Mac buried Pa beside Ma and the baby?" She bit her lip. "Well, at least we know where Pa ended up." She groaned as she rose and bent over to pick up baby Molly. "Time for bed, little one." She kissed the baby on the forehead.

Ben jumped up to grab the baby. "Dol. You know you aren't supposed to lift Molly in your condition. Let me put the girls to bed. You visit with your brother. Lizzie, give Mama and Uncle Frank a kiss goodnight."

"Thank you, hon. You are too good to me," she smiled at Ben, relieved to sit back down.

"Please, Mama. Can I stay up longer? I like Mr. Frank." She snuggled closer to him on the couch.

"Oh, all right. For a little bit, Missy."

Jenna took the baby from Ben. "I'll put Molly to bed, Ben. You visit with Dol and Frank. "Send Lizzie up in a while, and I'll read her a bedtime story."

Frank waited until Jenna was upstairs before he spoke. "You are very fortunate to have someone like Jenna wait on you hand and foot."

"Indeed. She is my gem. She has put a certain gleam in your eye, too, hasn't she?" Dol leaned back to stretch her over-taut stomach.

Ben noticed the strained look on her face as she tried to hide another wince. "Dol, you really should go to bed," Ben cautioned. "You've overdone it today."

"Oh, I'm fine, Ben – just an active child, that's all. Trying to kick the daylights out of me," she tried to chuckle and then grabbed her side. "I'll be all right if I sit quiet a little while longer."

Frank was glad Dolly had found a good, caring husband such as Ben.

Chapter 28 - The Funeral

Wednesday, the day of Mac's funeral, arrived too fast as far as Frank was concerned. There was still so much to search out. Someone had to know something about Guy. Maybe together, he and Dolly could figure out a plan.

He inspected the image in the mirror. Clean-shaven with his new white, crisp shirt tucked properly into his newly-hemmed trousers, the gray and black striped tie completed the look. He approved. He doubted anyone present would know him. He wasn't there to impress, but he still wanted to look decent.

He took a seat toward the back of the church and watched as the few people filed past the casket, each one stopping to pay their final respects. It was going to be a small funeral. Mac and his missus kept to themselves most of their years, so their friends were few. No family – except for me, if you could call me 'family,' Frank grimaced.

"May we sit next to you?" a lady's soft voice spoke in Frank's ear from behind.

Frank nodded and slid over a couple seats without looking up.

"It's good to see you again, Frank. So kind of you

to come back to honor Mr. Wheeler's memory." She spoke soft and low.

Surprised the woman knew his name, Frank looked at her and recognized her immediately. Even though her hair had grayed and a few wrinkles creased her forehead, it was undoubtedly Mrs. Johnson.

Anger? No. Rage. He felt it writhe up within his throat. He could taste it when he looked at her smiling face. He bit his lip as dark thoughts invaded his brain. How could she smile at him? She let my brothers die, his heart accused.

He moved several seats over so they could sit with wide space between them and kept his face to the front throughout the funeral.

When the service was over, Frank hurried toward the door. Mrs. Johnson followed close behind all the way to his car.

"Frank, wait. We saw you in church last Sunday. We're so glad to see you," said Helen Johnson. "You left so soon after Mike's accident. We didn't know how to find you."

He remained silent and sullen, muscles tensed at the mention of his brother's name.

"My husband and I would like for you to come to our house before you leave."

Frank looked at her with dark eyes. Suspicion arose in his thoughts.

"We have something special for you. Something you should have. Please?"

"I'll think about it," Frank said with a frown and a gruffness in his voice. He surprised himself.

He got into his car and sped off, leaving the Johnsons standing in its dust. Rage burned within him again, the ugly head of bitterness threatening to bite and overtake his soul.

Chapter 29 - Barn Discovery

Frank drummed the steering wheel as he maneuvered recklessly through town, unaware of where he was going. Stomach in knots, ready to empty its contents, he just drove.

Why would the Johnsons want to see me? What could they have to say? What would I want to hear?

Before he knew it, he was back at the farm. He stopped the car and stared out the window. It was a good place to think things over. No one would bother him here. He went inside the barn, found a bale to sit on and tried to process recent events: the pocket watch, Mac's letter, the funeral, Mike, the Johnsons, Simmons. How did it all tie together?

The turmoil over Mike's death tumbled within his being. He thought the matter had been settled in his soul. Seeing the Johnsons just brought the ugly bile to the surface again. His mind felt like a boxing match with aggressive thoughts pummeling accusations, and reason trying to referee.

He kicked at the straw as he walked through the barn, angry at Simmons, angry at the Johnsons. Angry at himself. Another kick and his foot hit something solid. He kicked away the straw and saw part of a broken, jagged handle to some sort of tool laying in the middle of the floor. He pushed aside more straw – the pitchfork? He gasped. How did I miss that before? The handle appeared stained.

That pitchfork was the same one he almost fell on when he jumped from the haymow as a kid. He dug through the straw until he found the fork. When he did, a chill went up his spine. The tines were coated with a black substance.

His heart skipped a beat. Frank got the broom and swept the loose straw into a pile. A curious dark stain covered part of the concrete floor. Feeling more frantic by the moment, he swept away the rest of the straw. Dizziness overcame him as he discovered the bloody drag marks all the way to the door Mac had seen. He licked his finger and touched the blackened substance on the tines. It turned his finger and the tines red.

What happened here? A chill ran up Frank's spine. Nothing good.

He stumbled into the dirt as he ran from the barn. A queasy, nauseous feeling overtook him. He suspected the worst.

It had to be.

Simmons.

Chapter 30 - Simmons Again?

Frank drove back to the Ryan home with heart pounding and mind reeling. What happened in that barn? Who was there? What did Mac find? Was Simmons there? What did Johnsons want with me? What could they have that I would want? What does Jenna think of me? What would Anne think?

Frank blinked his eyes to shake himself from the turmoil within. Almost missed his turn to the country road toward Dol's home.

As they enjoyed Jenna's fresh-baked lemon chiffon pie and coffee that evening, Frank brought up the subject which had bothered him all day.

"The Johnsons were at the funeral today, Dol. All I could think of was Mike. Couldn't even concentrate on Mac's eulogy. They want me to come over for some reason."

"Did they say why?"

"Said they have something special for me. Don't know what. Don't care. Don't want to see them. I...I can't do it."

She gave him a questioning look with a sisterly frown.

"Why should I?"

"You can't blame them, Frank. They must have done everything they knew to do. You must find it in your heart to forgive them...and forgive yourself, too."

Silence loomed in the room for a few moments as she waited for his response.

He frowned and stared at the floor. Didn't want to discuss this matter with her now. It was not the time, and he wasn't there to hear her advice. The only way around it was to change the subject. Cleared his throat and corralled his frustrations.

"I went back to the barn today after the funeral. Had to think. What I found put a chill up my spine. Found something else you should know about."

She raised her eyebrows. "You said before it looked like someone had lived there with all the empty cans and bottles, and you found the watch you believe belonged to Simmons. What else?"

"Well, for one, I found Guy's jacket – the one he had on the night we stayed in the barn. But that's not the scary part."

"Frank, stop," Jenna begged as she sat on the edge of her chair. "You're teasing now. Quit scaring us."

"It was scary, and almost made me vomit to think about it." He loved watching Jenna's black eyes grow large as he built suspense. He grinned.

"What, Frank? Tell us."

"Remember, I said it looked like there had been a fight and Mac's letter confirmed Pa and Simmons were fighting, but I found blood – lots of it. And, I found a bloody, broken pitchfork on the floor laying in a puddle of what appeared to once be a pool of blood."

"Now you are scaring *me*, Frank," Dol's eyes got large as she gasped. "How do you know it was blood?"

"Tasted it."

"Wonder whose it was?" Ben thought aloud.

"Well, whoever it was, there was more blood than just a nosebleed or a little fight. Someone was hurt there –hurt bad. Found the bloody drag marks all the way to the barn door Mac told about, too."

Dol put her hand to her mouth. "Do you think it was Simmons?"

"Wish I knew, Dol."

"Are you going to try to find Simmons, Frank?" asked Ben. "Think I would, if I were you."

"That's the lawyer in you, Benny," Dol tried to laugh – then winced as pain creased her face.

"I would want to get some answers from this strange man. Seriously Frank, you have to find out what really happened," Ben said.

"... and maybe, just maybe, you will find Guy in the process," Dol added.

"Well, as much as I hate the thought of it, I will consider it. Last I knew Simmons said he lived on a large farm the other side of the Missouri. That's what he told me long ago– if he were telling the truth.

"Maybe I will use the watch as an excuse to find him," Frank began to formulate the plan out loud. "Yeah," he nodded subconsciously, "that's what I'll do. Then I will make him explain himself. It will make him think twice to wonder how I ended up with it." He chuckled. "First though, I have to find him. The bartender told me he lived in Modamin, Iowa."

The baby pushed against Dol's belly hard enough for Frank to see. He noticed Dolly wince in pain.

"He is a strong one, isn't he?" Frank commented. He didn't know what else to say, but felt he had to say something.

"...and my soon-to-be son." Ben laid his hand lovingly on her stomach. He grinned at her, but she couldn't smile in return.

Dol looked to Ben for help as she struggled to rise from her chair. She let out a small cry as another pain grabbed at her back.

"It's getting late, Dol; you've been on your feet way too much today and you need to go to bed now," Ben frowned. He had seen that panicked look only a few days back.

"I'm fine," she lied and winced again. But her eyes told Ben he better help her lie down in a hurry. These pains were becoming more than she could bear.

Unaware, Frank excused himself and went to his room so absorbed in his thoughts, he did not realize Dol's labor pains had begun in frequent succession.

Chapter 31 - Night Time Scare

Frank lay awake several hours that night as his brain juggled thoughts of Pa, Mac, and Simmons. What was the connection? What really happened? Mac said he chased Simmons away because he and Pa were fighting over me. Did Simmons come back to finish the job?"

His thoughts tumbled back to why the Johnsons wanted to see him. He felt his body tense. I should probably see what they want – 'to bring closure' – as Anne would say. He sighed long and hard. Why can't I just let it go? Tried to force himself to sleep. Tired in spirit from the struggle against his will, Frank relented and tried to pray, but words would not come. Why did this have to be so hard? He gritted his teeth as he fought the darkness within.

"God, you know my thoughts and the condition of my heart, and I'm sorry I'm having so much difficulty with this. I need your help. Thank you for helping me find my sister, Dolly. If you want me to find Simmons, please guide my steps. And, if it's not too much to ask, please help me find Guy, too?"

Words from the preacher's sermon popped back into his mind, "If you hold bitterness and unforgiveness in your heart, the Lord will not hear you."

Frank tossed and turned in confusion, rolled over and then over again. Finally, he relinquished his will with a sigh of surrender. "And, please Lord, grant me grace and courage to visit the Johnsons. Help me to really forgive. Amen."

His body relaxed and he exhaled a breath of release. Soon he was in a deep sleep. He did not hear soft sobs of pain coming from the downstairs bedroom as Dol struggled in labor.

"Frank!" Ben's voice shouted up the stairs. "Frank – wake up! It's Dol. She's hemorrhaging."

Frank shot from his bed trembling, startled wide awake. He yanked on his pants and skipped every other step on the way downstairs.

He hurried to Dol's bedside and was shaken by her blood-soaked nightgown. Her face was drawn and pasty, agony written across her brow. A cry escaped her lips as she sat up in bed. She attempted to stand but fell back on the bed and groaned in pain.

"What can I do?"

"Help me carry her to the car, Frank. She can't walk." Ben clipped the orders.

Dol gave Frank a weak smile of gratefulness. "I'm glad you're here, Frankie." She pleaded with her eyes for Ben to be careful as he put his arms around her.

"Frank, get on the other side and lift."

"Benny," Dol screamed in pain, "Stop....the baby... coming. Now."

Jenna ran from her room at the sound of Dol's cries with a sleepy Lizzie close behind. Baby Molly awakened by all the commotion, screamed from her crib.

Lizzie's frightened eyes stared at her mother. "Mama! Is Mama gonna die?" She began to dart toward her mother, but Jenna caught her midway. The little girl wiggled and cried in Jenna's tight embrace as she tried to get free.

"Ben! What's wrong? What can I do?" Jenna's voice trembled in terror.

"Tend to the girls, Jenna." Ben attempted to sound calm, but his voice betrayed him. His stern eyes told her to get the child from the room, but Jenna was frozen in place, too scared to move. The baby would be a month early, and there was way too much blood loss. Something wasn't right. She searched Ben and Frank's faces for some type of reassurance, but none was given.

"Hold on, Sweets," Ben said in a throaty voice, "We'll get you to the hospital right away."

"Benny...I...can't...do...this," her weak voice came in short rapid breaths.

"Look at me, Dolores. You can. Concentrate. Breathe."

Frank was terrified. He remembered Mama's screams and the birth that killed her. He shifted Dol's right side against his shoulder, and she cried out in pain. He silently prayed for God's help and wisdom. If anyone needed it, they did right now.

"Benny...something's...wrong." She grabbed her lower abdomen. "...doesn't feel... right," she panted and grimaced in pain.

"Lift her gently, Frank," Ben's voice halted as he tried to calm his own nerves.

"Ben-neeee.... Do something!" She clawed at Ben's arm, her eyes wild.

"Frank. Get behind her. Support her back."

Frank's widened eyes showed the fright he felt. He remembered the foals and lambs he had helped Mac deliver. One had been born dead once, and the memory made him shudder. "Please God, help her. Help this baby," he prayed silently. "Help me."

"Don't worry, Sweets," Ben soothed, "I'm here."

Ben questioned Frank with his eyes. His shoulders heaved, his voice weak. "Look at me, Dol. You have to do this."

But Dol had already blacked out and slumped in Frank's arms.

Chapter 32 - Birth

"Dol, don't you die on me. Don't do this," Ben's worst nightmare stared him in the face. His face strained with fear, Ben's eyes pled for help.

"I don't know what to do, Frank."

"She's all right, Ben," Frank said. He hoped in his heart he was right. "She has only passed out from loss of blood. I can help if you will let me. I know what to do." He hoped he was right.

"Mama! Mama!" Lizzie cried, wild and wiggly in Jenna's arms.

"Your Mama's okay, little one." Frank felt a power beyond himself well up within him. He could help. He had to. He took Lizzie from Jenna and set her on the floor. Kneeling beside her, he spoke softly in her ear.

"Lizzie," he held her quivering body close so she couldn't see her mother, "I need you to help your Uncle Frank and your Mama. Can you do that?"

Her frightened eyes tried to look past him. Frank gently took her little face and focused it upon his. "I need you to be brave and help me. Will you do that?"

Lizzie sucked in her sobs with short gasps and nodded.

"Good girl. Go help Jenna get some towels," he looked toward Jenna who nodded in admiration and assent. "...and some hot water too and then call the doctor."

Jenna was glad for an excuse to help. "Your Mama will be just fine," Jenna said to the child as she took Lizzie's hand and led her out of the room. "Come help me get those towels." She was scared too. She tried to convince herself as much as the child. "Your daddy and Uncle Frank are here to help her. Come on, now."

"Ben, if you will allow me, I need to see if the baby is starting to crown."

Ben couldn't speak, only nodded, half in shock, half not knowing what else to do.

"Lie her back on the bed so her legs hang over the edge," Frank ordered. "Get behind her back, and put your arms around her and under her knees. Hold her tight in case she wakes up."

What Frank saw frightened him. "It's what I suspected. The baby is breech. I will need to turn him."

Jenna rushed back to the room with a bowl of hot water. Lizzie followed with all the towels her little arms would carry.

"The doctor is on the way," Jenna said.

"How long?" Frank raised his eyebrows.

"Close to forty minutes, if he has no trouble."

"Too long to wait. We have to do this now."

"Anything, Frank. Anything. Just save your sister," Ben's voice was hoarse with emotion.

Frank hurriedly washed his hands and arms. Dol was still unconscious – all the better.

"Jenna, take Lizzie back upstairs and see about Molly. Ben, stay where you are behind Dol to support her back. Keep holding her knees up," Frank barked the orders.

He pushed on Dol's lower abdomen to feel for the baby's bottom. Perhaps he could force the baby to turn on his own. The baby shifted just enough for Ben to fit his hand into the cavity.

Slowly and carefully, he reached to feel where the baby lay and the approximate placement of the umbilical cord. His mind flashed back to the lambs he helped to turn within their mother's wombs. I can do this. God, you have to help me do this. I need your wisdom.

Methodical small nudges moved the baby inch by inch. Almost there.

Dol's eyes fluttered as she awoke with a jab of pain. She felt pinned and jerked her body on instinct to escape. She let out a piercing scream as the child within her finally turned head down.

"Bennnneeeee...."

"I'm right here, Dol," Ben calmed. He held her tight, "Hang on."

"It's done," Frank announced. Beads of perspiration dotted his brow. "Now, Dol – I need you to push this big boy out."

She bore down and gritted her teeth, her face wet with sweat and tears.

"Good, Dol. Give me another one just like that. Push hard. Now."

Her face reddened as she bore down with all her might. With one final agonizing yelp, baby Ryan was born.

"The doctor's here," announced Jenna as she led him into the room.

"It's a boy!" Frank grinned as he held the baby up for all to see.

Dol sobbed with relief and gratefulness as she sunk into Ben's weary arms.

Chapter 33 - Talk with Jenna

Frank awoke the next morning to the smell of fresh cinnamon rolls wafting from the kitchen. He stretched long and hard, relieved from the tension he faced the night before. Although he'd only had a few hours' sleep, he felt good.

He was glad to know that Dol was safe in the hospital where the doctor could check her and the baby to make sure everything was all right. Frank filled with satisfaction with the commendation the doctor had given him the night before.

"Looks like I'm not needed here," the doctor said. "This baby has already been born."

The little guy gave his first cry before he had to be coaxed and lay quietly on his mother's bosom. Dol was exhausted by the labor and delivery, but smiled weakly.

"Doctor, I don't know what I would have done if my brother-in-law hadn't been here. He knew what to do," Ben admitted.

"It was his quick thinking that saved this baby and his mother," said the doctor. "The baby could have died had he not intervened when he did. And Ben, shame on you for not taking your wife to the hospital at her first signs of labor."

"You know how addle-brained I become when it comes to Dol's well-being," Ben said. "I thought it was only false labor like last week when we came to the hospital." Frank shook his head at Ben's lame excuse.

"Remember, I told you then this baby may come early. I could tell it may only be a matter of days – especially if Dolores didn't adhere to the strict bedrest as I instructed. Has she been up and about a lot? Under stress? Worked up over things?"

Ben nodded, eyes low. "Yes. There's been a lot happening in the Ryan household," he looked Frank's way. "I knew when I saw all the blood, it was too late. I'm glad Frank was here and knew what to do."

Ben, Ben, thought Frank. Yes, he's a good man for my sister. Good thing he's a lawyer and not a doctor. I'm glad I was here too, but I know I had help from above on this one. He looked up, nodded his head and said a silent thank you.

Frank arose, pulled on his jeans and T-shirt, and headed downstairs.

Jenna had coffee ready when he entered the kitchen. "My hero," she beamed as she handed him his mug. "Black – just as you like it."

Still in her pink robe, she struck him as the picture of the perfect homemaker.

"Frank, you were amazing last night. You saved Dol's life! How did you know what to do?"

Frank suddenly felt awkward and stammered for words. "Oh...it was nothing." He looked at the floor to search for the words that seemed to disappear from his mind. "Worked on a farm. You know. It just came to me."

"I prayed hard, Frank. I asked God to help you."

Frank nodded and smiled. "Yes, Jenna. I believe He did. I prayed very hard myself."

"The baby is real healthy. Seven pounds even. The doctor said Dol can come home in a day or two when she regains her strength."

"That's good. She lost a lot of blood, but she is strong. Think I'll give her a day to rest and then go see her tomorrow. Do you want to come along?"

"I would love to come with you, but someone needs to stay here with the girls. They will be up soon. Wanted to get the baking done before breakfast. Busy days ahead."

Frank raised his eyebrows in question.

"Well, Dol will be home in a day or so. I must get the house in order, wash the sheets and change the beds. And someone needs to keep up on the sewing business in her absence. I want everything to be ready when she comes home with the baby."

"You're a remarkable woman, Jenna. Dol is fortunate to have you here."

"I would do anything for her, Frank. She's closer than a sister." She poured herself a cup of coffee, and then sat down beside him at the table.

They sat in quiet reflection for a few moments simply enjoying each other's company and the taste of caramelized cinnamon rolls.

It feels good being with this woman. Feels right somehow. Frank admired her reflection in her cup.

She rose to put another hot roll on his plate and refill his coffee cup. She felt his eyes on her. The huge smile on his face gave him away. He winked when she looked at him.

"What?" she asked.

"Tell me again, Jenna. Why hasn't some lucky guy snatched you away?"

She gave him a little scowl, turned, and brushed away the question with her hand, her face crimson. She pretended to get something from the counter. Ignoring his question, she sat down beside him again and looked into his eyes. He grinned at her.

"Frank? Mind if I ask you a question?"

"Sure. Then will you answer my question if I answer yours?" he teased.

She hesitated. "Oh – just wondered. I know it's none of my business, but the other day when you told Dol the story about your brother and how he died..." she paused not sure how to word it.

Frank wrinkled his forehead. Where was this

going? He gave a small nod and waited for her to continue.

"Well, you blamed the Johnsons for doing nothing to help your brother."

Frank cleared his throat and unconsciously clenched his fist. "You're right, Jenna. It is none of your business." His tone changed; his smile was gone.

She paid no attention. "...but they were there, Frank. They did their best. They would have prevented the accident if it were at all possible. I'm sure they loved your brother."

"You weren't there. You don't know," his voice dark.

She spoke slowly, chose her words carefully. "You are right. I wasn't, and I don't know. What I do know is you have a choice to make: you can keep this—this ugly memory buried inside you and let every little thing remind you of the hurt. But—each time the scab is ripped off, another deeper scar is formed."

Frank looked at the floor with a scowl. "I suppose you think I should go see them and set things straight, right?"

Jenna laid her small hand on top of his clenched fist. The warmth and softness surprised him, and his anger began to melt.

"I don't want to pry, Frank, but it hurts me to see

you hurt. Maybe if you saw them and talked to them, you could move past this painful spot in your life. It may free your spirit in ways you don't realize."

Frank peered into her pleading eyes. "How would you know this, Jenna?"

Jenna pierced his soul with her black eyes. "Because I had to get past my hurts, too. When I was five years old, I was in a terrible accident with my parents. My father swerved to miss an oncoming car. The road was icy, and our car smashed into a tree. My father was killed instantly; my mother bled to death. That is how I got this ugly scar that makes me so unattractive. I had to learn to live with myself looking as I do, and to forgive the drunken driver who lived. It was his fault that I became an orphan. It was his fault that I look like this. I had to realize and accept the fact that God knows what's best for me. He has a plan. I only have to find it."

Frank relaxed his fist, and turned his hand over to hold Jenna's hand which covered his. An unbidden thought invaded his mind. Others have gone through hell too, and yet survived. His spirit softened, and it was reflected in his answer.

"Deep down, Jenna, I know what you say is true. God does have a plan. I only wish I could understand and see it." He closed his eyes tight. "I am trying. Really, I am."

"So, you will think about visiting the Johnsons before you leave the area?"

He admired her tenacity. "I will think about it." He backed his chair away from the table. "Today, though, I must find Sy Simmons. Have some old scores to settle with that man."

He looked into her face, and brushed her hair behind her ear with his hand. With his finger, he gently traced the scar on her face.

"Jenna, this scar does not make you unattractive. It defines you. It gives you character; it is what has made you strong...and very beautiful. Don't you ever let anyone tell you differently."

Her face glowed, and she tucked her chin. "You are sweet, Frank." She looked up into his face with a playful smile. "You scat now, Mr. Larue. I must get breakfast for the girls."

Inwardly, Jenna's heart warmed. He had noticed her.

Chapter 34 - Shaker's Bar

Frank inhaled deeply and dialed the number on the piece of paper he received from the bartender in Blair. He tried to formulate a good excuse to see Simmons without giving him the whole story.

"Hello?" a man's deep voice answered.

"Sy Simmons?" Frank asked.

"Yes. Who's this?"

"Someone interested in seeing you. I have something that belongs to you."

Curiosity raised Simmons' voice a notch. "What could you have of mine that I'd want?" Simmons' mind raced through his list of deals gone wrong, but couldn't recollect any threatening ones recently.

"How about a gold pocket watch?"

"Who did you say this was?" Simmons' voice rose another couple notches.

"I didn't. Where can we meet?"

Simmons fidgeted. What had become of that watch? Silence.

"You there, Simmons? Name the place. I'll meet you."

The farm won't do. It would have to be more neutral, more public. Had to think quick. "Corner of Elm and Dawn. Shaker's Bar in Blair. When?"

"Today. Noon. Be there. I'll bring the watch. It will be on the bar in front of me. I'll be wearing a brown baseball cap."

Frank arrived a half hour early at Shaker's Bar and Grill. He took a seat on a barstool, placed the gold pocket watch on the bar, ordered a club soda and waited. Chest tight and breaths heavy, he was nervous about this meeting. Would Simmons remember him?

Twelve o'clock came, and Simmons had not yet showed. Frank grew fidgety. Where was he? Would he back out? Seated at the bar, he could see whoever came in the door on the mirror-backed wall in front of him. He resituated his brown cap, and ordered another drink.

Close to 12:30, Frank saw a man in bib overalls and flannel-checked shirt enter the bar. It was Simmons – not the fancy suit-clad Simmons he met years before who claimed to be his father, clean-shaven and cologne-splashed. This man was unshaven and had a salt and pepper beard and mustache. But no mistake. It was him.

Frank's mind slid back to the day Simmons told him to be ready – ready to leave everything and move in with him at his farm. Said he'd better be ready to go, no questions asked. Fast forward a few months to the day he really did come. Frank's mind spun. That day changed the course of my life forever. I wasn't about to let Mac sell me to a stranger. Frank felt the anger rise as a bitter taste swelled within his throat.

Simmons saw the young man with the brown baseball cap at the bar, his back towards the door. The pocket watch lay on the bar in front of him. He felt a queer fear – a memory hidden with that watch had long been buried. What was it? Where had it been?

He sat down on the barstool beside Frank, picked up the watch and turned it over in his hand. His initials, SOS, were engraved on the back.

"Sylvester Orville Simmons." He bit his lip as he paused. "Yep. Looks like you've found my watch. Been missing it quite a spell. Where did you find it?"

Frank turned to face the man, and removed his cap.

Sy Simmons' jaw dropped as he reared back, eyes wide.

"Timothy?"

Frank glared and did not smile. "I go by Frank," his voice terse.

Simmons shook his head and blinked several times, as if unable to process what his eyes revealed.

"It is you. No mistaking that." He spat his chew on the floor. "I'd know you anywhere – though you've grown up some."

Frank struggled to keep his voice low and calm to maintain control. He tapped the watch in Simmons' hand.

"So tell me. How did you lose this watch?"

"What do you mean?" Simmons looked from the watch into Frank's fiery eyes.

"You know what I mean," his voice became more intense. "Tell me what you know about my Pa, and how you lost your watch – in – our – barn, Simmons."

Frank watched Simmons' eyes jerk from the watch to his face with a look of alarm as the memory flooded back. His hands trembled, but he kept shaking his head. "Don't know."

"Don't tell me you don't know," Frank pressed. "I can see it in your eyes."

Simmons looked down to avoid Frank's angry glare.

"You were in our barn – fighting with my Pa. Admit it." Frank slammed his fist on the bar so hard it made Simmons jump. A few folk close by began to stare. He grabbed Simmons by the collar. "Tell me. Now."

Simmons pulled down on Frank's hands and pushed him back. He frowned with a new gruffness and glared at Frank with squinty eyes.

"Are you threatening me?"

"Like you threatened my Pa?" Frank yanked his hands away from Simmons' grasp, rebounded with a blow to the old man's face, and knocked him to the floor.

"Stop. Now." the bartender warned, "I'm calling the police."

With disregard Simmons countered, "Swear I don't know what you're talking about." He lunged at Frank's legs and Frank fell to the floor. "You fight just like a sissy - just like your pa."

Frank's face flushed in fury. He jumped on top of the big man and began to club his face. Simmons swung back and split Frank's lip.

Everyone in the bar turned to watch the scene unfold as voices became louder, actions bolder.

"I warned you two," shouted the bartender as the bouncer shoved them out the door.

Simmons landed another blow to Frank's head which sent him sprawling to the sidewalk. He bent down and grabbed Frank by the collar for another punch.

Frank wasn't about to be defeated. He kicked Simmons hard in the groin and doubled the man to his knees.

"I want answers, Simmons," Frank demanded, now on his feet.

"Break it up you two or get thrown in jail," the sheriff warned as he came toward them.

"Get up," Frank ordered with a kick to Simmons' side.

"I warned you," growled the sheriff as he pulled Frank away from another kick and yanked his arms behind him. "You're both going to the slammer tonight."

Frank stared at Simmons still doubled over on the sidewalk.

"You're a scrappy one," hissed Simmons as he spat on the ground and scoffed, "just like your old man. Look just like him, too."

So there it was. He had lied all along. What else had he lied about?

Chapter 35 - Answers in a Cell

"Just like old times," Simmons hissed, "sitting in jail with a Larue."

"I'm nothing like my father," Frank shot back.

"Oh, you're more like him than you know."

Frank gave him an angry stare and bit his lip. "Tell me. What was your pocket watch doing in our barn?"

Simmons thought quickly, "Not my watch."

"It's your initials. Checked it out and said so yourself."

"Nope – your pa won it off me on a bet."

"So you did know Pa then."

"Yah, I knew your pa all right. LeRoy was quite the gambler and drinker. He was a lady's man, too. Sorry to bust your bubble and all."

Frank, worn down by lies, sat back on the cold cell bench. He shrugged his shoulders. How much could he really believe? Did it even matter now?

"LeRoy and I go way back. Met your pa across the street at Shaker's bar many years ago. Sat at the same card table. Terrible gambler and a worse cheat. Won lots of money off that oaf," he bragged. "Got stupid when he got some liquor in him."

"Liked his women too. Fought over Lilly Sue lots.

We both ended up in jail many times," Simmons roared and spat on the floor.

"Found him at McGraff's in Tekamah once, and we got into quite a tangle. Landed both of us in jail," he snorted. "After that, met up at least once a month for a card game over the years. Found it was a good way for me to win money."

Frank brooded as the news soaked in.

"Once I saw your brother, Guy, come to pick up your pa from jail. Husky boy for a young teen. Looked like a good hard-working kid. Liked what I saw. Knew he would be a good fit for my farm."

Frank's ears perked up. What about Guy? "But why did you want me? Why did you say you were my pa? Said you'd found Guy and wanted to find Dolly. Told quite a tale about you and Ma – but you didn't want me for a son, did you? You lied." Frank glared at the older man who sat unmoved and straight-faced across from him.

Simmons ignored the question and looked at the ceiling. "I waited and waited the day I came to pick you up. Mrs. Wheeler had packed your stuff in a small flour sack. Saw you walking up the road, so I chatted with Mr. Wheeler while we waited. He feigned a concerned look, "When you didn't show up, I got worried."

"You mean, you got angry. You just wanted me for your farmhand, didn't you? You bought me."

Simmons raised his eyebrows in surprise. "Ha. Bought you?" He chuckled and spat again.

"Quit lying, Simmons. I saw Mac give you money. Admit it. He sold me to you."

Simmons laughed again. "A kid with a huge imagination. Yeah, I took money from Wheeler—for a sack of grain for his horses. Had nothing to do with you. I was angry you didn't show up. I hoped I'd find you at the barn, where I picked up Guy."

Guy? With Simmons? Frank eyeballed the man. He felt dizzy at the news.

Simmons saw the unspoken question. "No. He's gone. Don't know where. Ran off, I reckon. Thought he came back to look for you – thought I'd catch you both." Simmons shrugged. "Made him tell me where you lived. Needed more help on the farm; besides, your pa owed me."

"Wait. Guy lived with you?" Frank stood to his feet in shock.

"Worked for me – paying off your pa's debt."

Frank scowled and shook his head. "I don't understand."

Simmons shrugged his shoulders. "Your Pa owed me," he repeated.

"When Larue couldn't pay up, he told me to take Guy. May have been drunk as a skunk when he told me to let his kid pay off his debt, but I didn't care if he was drunk or not. Said to get you and Dolly too.

Made Guy go work for me on my farm. Your brother didn't want to go and didn't want to stay. Thought if you were there, he would work better, and then I'd have me two ranch hands. Dolly would only make it better 'cuz I needed a good cook. Looked, but never found her."

And I'll never tell you, Frank said under his breath.

"Guy didn't want to tell me where you were, but I pushed until he gave you up." Simmons spat again. "Thought I'd got a great deal – two for one."

"Guy worked for me a while. When I came to get you, Guy took off. Thought he might have come back to warn you or to see his pa. Had to get you to come with me one way or the other, so I made up the story about your ma leaving me."

"So, you lied to me," Frank sneered. "I knew it all along."

"Seemed like a good plan at the time," he sniffed.

The whole story was hard to process. So Pa didn't only abandon us, he gave us up and sold us. He shook his head. Frank's heart felt heavy. Felt abandoned all over again. Could he believe what this man said now?

A few long moments passed before Frank dared to ask the next question. Baiting him, he asked.

"Were you in a fight with my Pa?"

"Sure. Lots of fights. That's what landed us in jail

all the time."

"I mean at our barn, Simmons."

"Don't even know where your barn is, kid," he lied as his eyes shifted to the corner of the cell.

"Quit lying, old man. You just said you knew where it was. You were there, and your watch was on the barn floor."

"Told you, your Pa owned my watch. Won it on a bet."

"And you've never been to our barn?"

"Never," Simmons shouted and spat on the floor.

"You're a liar, Simmons," Frank barked back. "Mac saw you there – in a fight with Pa."

Simmons' nostrils flared, and he began to laugh in scorn. "So you talked to Mac, huh?" He shifted his weight on the cell bench, more agitated. "Hmmmm."

"Said he had to pull you two apart before you killed each other."

Simmons scratched his grey beard and spat on the floor and studied the puddle it had become.

"Yeah," he finally admitted. "I went to the farm spitting mad to look for you and Guy because now instead of two workers, I had none. Wanted you both, but LeRoy didn't know where any of you kids went." He spat.

"Demanded he pay up and give me back my watch. He refused and yelled back. Always was a scrapper," he snorted. "Long story short, we got into a big tussle. He was a sorry drunk who liked to fight. And you're right. Wheeler found me there. Pulled us apart and told me to hightail it."

"So...?" Frank paused long as he stared Simmons in the eye. "Tell me. Did you kill him?"

Shocked, Simmons sat up straight in his seat. "What? Kill who? What are you talking about?"

"My Pa. He was found dead in the barn. You admitted you were there; it was your watch at the barn. It had to be you. The watch was not far from the pitchfork. Blood stains all over the floor."

He scowled with shifty eyes. Though his voice remained calm, it raised in pitch; he seemed unnerved.

"News to me, kid. LeRoy was still breathing when I left him. Beat up and drunk, yes. But alive. Gave your pa one last punch and left. He passed out in the straw. Don't know nothing about any bloody broken pitchfork. That is the honest truth."

Chapter 36 - Uncle Frank

"Uncle Frank, what happened to you?" Lizzie pointed at his bruised chin and bloody lip. "Does it hurt?"

Jenna inspected his face with curiosity as he came through the door. "We were worried sick over you. Wondered about you all night." She brought a warm, wet washcloth and dabbed at his lip. "Where were you?"

"Jail," Frank smirked.

"Jail? Frank Larue – shame on you." She pressed harder on the washcloth making him flinch.

"Ow." He pulled back and grinned.

"Why were you in jail?"

"Found Simmons. Got answers." He pointed to the bruise on his chin with a pouty face. He enjoyed her special attention.

"You are a scoundrel," she gave him a playful pat on the sore spot. "Now go get cleaned up and presentable. Your sister is due home within the hour. You have a new nephew to meet, and I have girls to feed."

He took a quick shower and put on clean clothes when he heard the door shut downstairs.

"We're home," called Ben.

"Calling Dr. Larue," Dol yelled up the stairs. "Come meet your namesake. Timothy Benjamin is here."

The baby boy had fine black hair the color of his father's and a round chubby face with dimples like Dol's. She lifted the baby toward Frank.

He wrapped his arms around the tiny bundle, awed by the child. "You named him after me?"

"You and his father. I owe his life – and mine – to both of you. I am so glad you were here to help me bring him into the world."

"He's a wonder, Dol." Frank marveled at the creation asleep in his arms.

Lizzie tugged to pull down Frank's arm. "I want to see my brother, Uncle Frank."

Molly crawled over to her mother's leg and pulled herself up. "Come girls, help Mama put your new brother in his crib." Jenna took the baby from Frank and went upstairs with Dol.

"Frank, how did you get the big lip?" Ben tapped his chin after Dol left the room.

"Found Simmons. He and I had a heart to heart," Frank chuckled.

"Looks like he did a little more than that."

"You should see him. Anyway, found the answers I needed to hear. Can't wait to talk to you and Dol about it. It's almost too farfetched to believe."

"Did he know who you were?"

"Oh, yeah – right away, and it almost scared the liver from him. Caught him in his lies."

Frank shared the encounter with Simmons over lunch.

"And he wanted to find me too?" Dol asked, "...to be a cook for his men? How ridiculous. I would have never agreed no matter what he claimed."

"He thought he found a whole work crew from the Larue family. Planned to make Pa pay one way or another. He apologized, although it didn't sound sincere – simply spouted words."

"Well, I am glad for once that I was in the orphanage where he couldn't find me or the girls," Dol breathed a sigh of relief. "I'm glad Guy got away from him and that he never got to you. Who knows what he would have made you do? Wonder where Guy disappeared to? And I still wonder about Gracie and Josie."

"There has to be a way we can locate them. Maybe you could ask at the orphanage again, Dol. They may tell you now since several years have passed."

Dol wrinkled her forehead in doubt. "Could try, I guess. And where would we even start to look for Guy?"

"That is the question, dear sister. We will have to pray God shows us the way."

After the children were in bed for the night, Ben, Dol, Jenna, and Frank settled in the living room for coffee and conversation.

"Frank, did you ask Simmons about the fight with Pa?"

"Yeah. He admitted they fought, but said it was over the pocket watch. Said he knocked Pa out cold, then left." Frank rubbed the sore spot on his chin. "He seemed nervous. Kept looking at the floor, then for the guard. The man's a liar, and I don't trust him."

"Do you think he did it? Do you think he killed your Pa?" Ben asked.

"It makes me wonder. Mac said they were quarreling over me, not the watch."

"I'll have to leave for Wisconsin tomorrow morning. Need to get back to the church and to my job. There is only one more loose end to tie up."

Dol wrinkled her forehead. "You've found me — the most important part," she grinned. "You've met your family here and helped introduce your nephew into the world. You've said your goodbyes to Mac Wheeler and met a wonderful single girl," she looked over and gave Jenna a sisterly smile.

"You found Simmons and dealt with him, and found Pa. What else could there possibly be?" She tapped her finger to her chin, and raised her eyebrows at him, although she knew the answer.

Jenna shot Frank a knowing glance.

"Oh, yes." Dol paused long. "...the Johnsons. Are you going to follow through and meet with them?"

Frank nodded. "Yes. I had a long night in jail to think things over." He grinned sheepishly. "Didn't sleep much. Plan to call and set up a time to see them before I leave."

Dol and Jenna both nodded their approval. "Good. We will pray it all goes well. You will be relieved, you'll see."

Frank was doubtful – yet, there was still hope. He prayed it would go well too.

Chapter 37 - The Meeting

Jenna was right, Frank pondered on his drive to the Johnsons. She echoes a lot of Anne's words. I have to get this part of my life over and get past this ache.

The bitterness in his gut ate him alive on the drive there. Worries of how he would approach the subject of his brother, what he would ask, what they would say, where they would go from there. Through Dol's and Jenna's persuasion, he knew it was the right thing to do. He hoped the meeting would quell the anxiety he felt within.

He pulled into the drive of the Johnson's huge two-story corner estate, turned off the ignition, and sat. This is the place he heard the Christmas story for the first time. He grinned in spite of himself. How funny the Johnson girls looked dressed in their house robes reenacting the birth of Jesus. He closed his eyes and smiled.

Jesse's last Christmas was spent here. His smile faded. Christmas dinner was the last time he had with Jesse there. Jesse had been too sick and weak to even eat. Didn't last long after that.

Frank straightened himself to reality. He squared his shoulders, and forced one foot in front of the other toward the white colonnade entrance. With his heart in his throat, he lifted the brass ring to knock. They were expecting him, and he was on time.

"Welcome, Frank," Helen Johnson greeted him with a smile. Her welcome sounded earnest. "We are glad you agreed to come. Joe is waiting for you in the den."

He followed her to the room where the children's Bible club met — the place he first heard about Jesus – who, for some silly reason, he believed to be the name of Mary Johnson's doll.

Joe Johnson stood as Frank entered the room, shook his hand and invited him to sit.

"May I get you a coffee or soda, Frank?" Mrs. Johnson asked.

"No, no. Nothing, thank you." He sat on a plush chair in a room surrounded by bookcases. He crossed with his arms and wondered where to start.

Mrs. Johnson settled herself beside her husband on the sofa. Her eyes displayed a softness and empathy for Frank. It made him feel nervous and out of place. How can I get the answers I need to hear? Thankfully, he found he didn't have to ask.

"We have wanted to get in touch with you for quite some time, Frank," Mr. Johnson began.

Mrs. Johnson interrupted, "But first, we want you to know how sorry we are about your brothers.

We loved them like our own sons. Mary and Sarah thought of them as their younger siblings. We would have done anything for them."

Frank felt his body tense and his hands tighten. Breathed a quick prayer and forced his muscles and mind to relax and stay calm. This was harder than he thought. He stared at the floor and nodded for them to continue.

"She is right, Frank. We loved those boys dearly. We did everything possible for little Jesse – took him to the finest doctors in Lincoln, gave him the best medicines. He was simply too sick and weak when he came to us. There was nothing more we could do for him."

"And Michael's tragedy was almost too much for us to bear. We blamed you for the longest time. God had to deal with our anger towards you," said Mrs. Johnson.

Frank's head jerked up in surprise. "Blamed me? Why would you blame me?"

"Well...you brought the horse to town that day. It was Easter Sunday. You should have been in church with us, not working. Michael had invited you to come to church with us, but instead you brought the horse and cart to town. We had a very hard time with that. If you hadn't been there, or would have come with us, our Michael would still be alive today."

Frank was stunned. He felt as if one hundred pounds of weight had been dropped on his chest. He had never thought about it that way. Instead, he had blamed them. He felt drained, yet his eyes brimmed as his heart bled.

"We needed to see you so we could clear our consciences and cleanse our spirits. We want you to know that we forgive you. After Mac Wheeler started attending church, we learned what kind of life you had there, living in the same house with Irma Wheeler. You could only obey what you were told, and do whatever you were allowed. You had to survive. Mac explained it all to us. It wasn't your fault Frank. Michael's accident couldn't be prevented. Some things just happen."

"And we are sorry we held it against you for so long," added Mrs. Johnson. "We no longer have bad thoughts about you. God helped us forgive and get past our resentment. He helped us go on."

Frank raised his chest with a heavy sigh. He cleared his throat. "If you don't mind, I could take that drink of water now." His voice was raspy, full of emotion. It was time to clear the air.

Mrs. Johnson nodded and rose to get it. While she was out of the room, he looked toward Joe Johnson with surrender in his spirit.

"And, I have held it against you." He blinked away the tears. "...couldn't you have done more...to save Mike?"

With tears in his own eyes, Mr. Johnson spoke softly. "Frank, I chased the run-away horse and tried to stop it, and then I ran to find the doctor. There was nothing more I could have done. The damage to Michael's body was too severe. His bones were crushed. By the time the doctor arrived, it was too late. Helen was with him to the end – every minute. Your brother did not die alone. His last words were 'tell Frankie that Jesus loves him, and I'll see him someday in heaven.'"

The words rang true and broke Frank's heart. He put his head in his hands and wept. "It should have been me. It should have been me. I should have been killed instead."

"There was nothing you could have done, Frank. You were only a young boy. The horse spooked at the lightning and thunder."

"Then maybe it's God's fault," Frank said in a low, soft voice. "He made it rain." He felt tired and beaten.

"Oh, Frank. Dear Frank," Helen Johnson laid her hand on his shoulder. "No one can be blamed – not you, not us, not God. Michael simply went home earlier than we all wanted, that's all."

Spirit broken, Frank sobbed quietly. Mrs. Johnson brought him tissues, and he wiped his eyes. He realized for the first time that they had done their best.

A few moments of silence passed as Frank regained his composure. "Will you pray for me?" He choked out the words.

"Frank, the Bible says God is close to those who are brokenhearted, and toward those whose spirit feels crushed. Today, that is you. He wants to heal your heart and spirit. Do you agree?"

Frank nodded, head down. Joe Johnson prayed a prayer of reconciliation and healing as Helen stood by his side. He continued to nod as Mr. Johnson prayed. Frank's shoulders relaxed as the burden lifted and defenses crumbled. He looked up at the couple standing before him with tear-streaked eyes. He gave a weak and forgiving smile. They were kind and good people. "I forgive you Mr. Johnson, Mrs. Johnson. I'm sorry I held Mike's death against you for so long. Please forgive me?"

"Of course, Frank." Helen Johnson gave him a hug. "Of course."

Frank wiped his eyes again and exhaled a breath of relief. "You know, he was quite the little preacher," Frank mused. "Told me about Jesus every chance he got. Mike made learning the Bible exciting and encouraged me to find my own way to God. And then..." he sighed long, "he laid down his life to save me. Today, I finally understand that."

The Johnsons smiled and nodded. "Mike's life

was not in vain."

Frank stood to go. "I must get back to my sister's and pack. I leave tomorrow for home."

Helen Johnson jumped from her chair as if she were poked with a pin. "Wait, Frank. I just remembered. There is one more thing before you leave. One of the most important things and I almost forgot. It is why we wanted you to come here in the first place. Wait right there."

Curious. Frank looked to Joe Johnson for explanation. He simply smiled knowingly.

She hurried back into the room waving an envelope in her hand. "We have been saving this letter for three, no—almost four years now. We contacted Mr. Wheeler, but he didn't know where you had gone. Said you ran away and hadn't heard from you. Since we prayed to find you someday, we kept the letter—unopened."

"Who is it from?"

"That's the question, Frank. We don't know. It may be too late to give it to you now, but all the same, it is addressed to you. It may be important – or it may be nothing."

Frank inspected the envelope. "Looks official with a government seal and all. Does seem important but there is no return address. The postmark says California. I don't know anyone from there. Thank you for keeping it all these years. And thank you for your prayers and for not giving up on me."

He shook their hands at the door. "It has done me a world of good to see you today. I almost let my pride win out and keep me away. Glad I didn't."

Letter in hand, Frank walked to his car with a new sense of freedom in his soul. The evening sunset seemed to be struck with more brilliant hues than he had ever seen before.

Chapter 38 - The Letter

Frank couldn't wait to get back to Dol's. The thirty minute drive was filled with relief, thanksgiving, and yet more questions. Who was in California? He knew of no one. It was puzzling.

He entered the kitchen through the back door to the aroma of roasting beef, his favorite, but it did not deter him. He had to know what was inside the envelope.

"Frank, are you all right?" Jenna asked as he hurried past her without saying hello. He nodded absentmindedly without looking at her and headed upstairs to his room. Not even little Lizzie could get his attention.

"Why is Uncle Frank mad at me?" Lizzie asked with a frown.

"Oh, he's not mad at you, Missy. Just in a hurry for some reason. Must have lots on his mind." It made her worry too. She sensed an urgency she couldn't place. Yet, there appeared to be a peace on his face. She couldn't wait to talk to this man she had begun to love, but now was not the time.

Frank sat on the edge of his bed and tore open the yellowed envelope. What he read created even more of a conundrum. He knew right away Dol would want to read it. He would show her after supper when they could talk without the children interrupting. This would be his last night at the Ryans. Together they had to devise some sort of plan.

"Took care of things at the Johnsons today, Dol," Frank began. "They — and God — helped me see things a whole different way."

"I'm so glad, Frank."

He went on to explain the encounter. "Before I left, they gave me a letter, Dol—a letter from Guy."

Her eyes widened in surprise. "Guy's alive? Where?"

"I don't know. He was alive when he wrote it a few years back. Here, read it for yourself."

> *"Frank,*
> *We were told to write family before we left. This is the only address I remember. The Johnsons will get it to you.*
> *Owe you an explanation. You need to know about Pa. So sorry.*
> *Looked for him everywhere. Checked the bars, checked the jails. Looked all over the county. Searched for days but didn't find him.*

Headed back to the barn on the back roads one night and found Pa's truck in the ditch. He'd passed out - looked like he'd hit his head. Barely alive. Dirty, smelly, and drunk. Not sure how long he'd been there.

Got the truck out of the ditch, drug Pa into the back and brought him back to the barn. Fixed it up for shelter. Stole food to eat.

When Pa sobered up he began to ask questions. Wanted to know where all you kids were. Threatened me. Beat me. Told him I wouldn't tell until he said sorry. He said he'd never say sorry. You know how angry and mean he got.

One day a man showed up to get money from Pa. Saw the guy in jail with him once. Pa told him he was broke. Told him to let me work off his debt. Didn't want to go, but he made me. No choice. Worked on his farm close to three years. Tried to run, but he always forced me to come back. Threatened to get Dolly or you if I didn't stay.

Told me Pa gambled to pay off his debt but always lost. He owed lots of angry people who wanted their pay. The guy said Pa told him to take you too, but didn't know where you were. Beat me till I told him. Sorry, Frankie.

When he came to get you, I ran to warn you. Headed for the barn first. I was so mad. Asked Pa why he gave us up and sold us off?

Didn't answer, drunk again. Swung at me like usual. Knocked me down, but this time I punched back. Swung at my face full-force with his fist. I ducked and then swung back. My fist connected with his jaw. Hard. Lunged at me again. Wouldn't back off. Made me furious. Grabbed the first thing close and struck him hard in the head. Knocked him to the floor. The huge gash in his head bled like a stuck pig. Threw the pitchfork down, but couldn't stop kicking him.

So scared. I'm as bad as him, Frank. Scared I killed him. Didn't mean it. Kicked the straw over the bloody mess and ran.

Today I leave for the war. Heading out to sea on a ship to who knows where. Have to get far away. Maybe I'll get the just punishment I deserve. --Sorry. Guy.

Tears welled up within Dol's eyes as she scowled at the paper in her hands, visibly shaken. "So Guy killed Pa?" her voice incredulous.

"He thought he did," Frank said. "I can't believe it either."

"Wait," Ben spoke. "You said before it looked like bloody drag marks led to the barn door, right?" His lawyer's mind kicked into gear.

Frank nodded. "Mac said he found Pa by the barn door, like he dragged himself there. I saw them too."

"The letter says Guy kicked straw over Pa's body and left him lay – in the middle of the barn – where you found the pitchfork. I don't think he killed him; maybe only knocked him out."

"Then who?" Dol questioned.

"What about Mr. Wheeler?" wondered Ben. "Would he have had any cause to harm LeRoy?"

"Not Mac. He was too kind."

"Even in self-defense? What if your Pa was drunk enough to attack Mac?"

Dol nodded her agreement. "You know what a maniac Pa became when he was drunk. His anger was out of control."

Frank agreed.

"Maybe Pa attacked him in a drunken rage. Maybe Mac killed him by accident in self-defense."

"Good thought, Dol. But Mac would have

admitted to it if it were an accident...but Mac is not here to ask. I would bet Simmons is the culprit. He came back to confront Pa, and it went south." Frank's face screwed into a frown as he assembled the puzzle in his brain.

"...the pitchfork. That's it, Ben. The pitchfork was bloody and broken when I found it. Guy's letter says he hit Pa with it, but then threw it down. Doesn't say anything about it being broken."

"Okay...so, where are you going with this?"

"Simmons."

Both Dol and Ben squinted at Frank with mystified looks.

"Yes? Go on..."

"Simmons also said he didn't know anything about a bloody broken pitchfork."

The light in Ben's eyes lit up as he began to nod.

"Ben, I never told him it was broken – or bloody."

Dol's eyes widened with the knowledge.

"He told me he left him alive, but I don't trust the guy. He's a down right liar."

"But how do we prove it, Frank? And how do we find Guy to let him know he's innocent?" Dol asked.

"That's where I come in, Sweets," Ben narrowed his eyes with thoughts already swirling in his head. "I think there may be a way."

"Now that's my lawyer-husband talking,"

admiration in her voice and eyes.

"Frank," said Ben, "you may have to stay over another day. Do you think you can get Simmons to meet you one more time?"

Chapter 39 - Setting the Trap

"Called Simmons. He agreed to meet again tomorrow. Told him I wanted closure."

"Good," replied Ben. "He'll think you're alone. Sheriff Stevens agreed to meet me there around 4:00 p.m."

Frank nodded. So far, things were going as planned. He prayed they could trap this slippery fox in his own words.

Frank entered Shaker's bar squinting to find the man. Simmons beckoned to Frank from the back table where the lights were low. Frank sauntered to the dimly lit corner and extended his hand. "Thanks for meeting me here. Wanted to see you one last time before I head back home."

The older man glared in suspicion. "And where's home?"

"North. A long ways north."

"Took the liberty of ordering us drinks," Simmons said, "for old times' sake." He laughed nervously.

"Good." Get good and drunk before I start asking questions, Frank thought.

"Have to settle some things, Simmons. That is what this trip back here was all about. Want you to know there are no hard feelings."

Simmons narrowed his eyes, looked into his empty glass and ordered another. He drummed the table with his fingers. "That's it? All's forgiven?"

Frank nodded. "That's it. Want it settled, that's all." Ben and Bob came in the door, noted where Frank was seated and nonchalantly worked their way to the bar. They gave Frank a silent nod. He saw them out of the corner of his eye and gave a slight nod back.

"Hey Ben...imagine finding you here. Hi, Bob." Frank waved them over to the table. "Join us. You don't mind do you, Simmons?" Frank forced a smile at the man.

"Not at all. Call me Sy. The more the merrier. We were about to order another round." He flagged the waitress with his empty glass.

"Sy, these are my good friends, Ben and Bob." Since both were in plain clothes, Simmons was none the wiser that an attorney and a sheriff joined him for a pointed conversation. He shook their hands, feeling a little safer with more bodies present. Not noticing Frank's still full glass, he ordered another drink and his tongue became looser, his brain more numb.

The waitress came over to refill his glass and take drink orders from the other men.

"Lily Sue, meet LeRoy's son, Frank." He slapped

Frank on the back.

This is Lily Sue? The lady my Pa fought over? Frank mused. With ink-black dyed hair and painted face, she gave the appearance of a true floozy. She gave Frank a wide grin of approval behind the bright red lipstick revealing a couple missing teeth.

"Well, I'll be. If it ain't LeRoy resurrected."

Simmons shot her an irritated look.

She ran her fingers through Frank's curly hair. "Well he does, Sy – just like him. Look at all this red hair...curly too, just like LeRoy's. I was always such a sucker for..."

"Okay, okay, Lilly Sue," Simmons interrupted and smacked her bottom. "Go get my drink already."

Frank laughed it off and waited until she walked away.

He spoke to the men. "Sy here, was good buddies with my Pa back in the day. Played cards with him here at this very table, isn't that right, Sy?" He returned the slap.

"Where I met him," he nodded. "After your ma died, we got together more often for a binge. LeRoy tried to forget his misery in the bottle. Blubbered and complained when he was drunk. Said he didn't know what to do with all you kids. Told me how much trouble it was and wished he could get rid of you."

"Did you ever go to the Larue's farm?" asked Ben.

"Yeah. Followed him home one time – all the way to Tekamah. Owed me money, and I was bound and determined to get it one way or another. Found him in McGraff's bar there, and we got into quite a tangle. Ended up in jail for the night, both of us beat up pretty bad." His laugh was sarcastic. It was all a big joke.

"Thought you told me that fight was over your watch," said Frank.

He shrugged his shoulders. "Yeah. Well, maybe. Went back to get the watch. LeRoy owed me."

"But, you told me you never went back," Frank scratched his head and tried to act perplexed.

Simmons laughed nervously, his voice high.

"So LeRoy gambled all his money away, huh?" asked Ben.

"Haw, won lots of money off that old cuss," he spat. "Gamble the shirt off his own back, he would. When he ran out of money, he pawned whatever he had on hand." He began to chortle at his own joke – "like the ring on his finger or his wife's, ain't that right, Lily Sue?" He smacked her bottom as she set another glass before him.

"Only had to give him a few bucks." She flashed her finger in front of Frank's nose and giggled.

Frank's rage billowed within. He tightened his lip

and bit his tongue. He couldn't let his anger control him now. He gave Ben a nod.

"Heard he even gave up his own sons to pay his debt," said Ben.

Sy Simmons roared. "Ain't that somethin'? Can you believe it? Said 'take Guy...and Frankie too. Let 'em work off my debt.' Would have worked too, if this guy here," he slapped Frank's back again, "would have cooperated and just came with me." He roared with derisive laughter. "You know that's right, don't you, Frank?"

"And what happened when they didn't come, Sy?" Bob wanted to know.

"Whaddaya mean?"

"You went back to collect your due after Mac Wheeler told you to leave. Angry and upset, you got into a bad fight with LeRoy – a deadly fight that didn't end well. How am I doing, Simmons?" Ben hammered. "Coming close?"

"Whaddaya mean?" he asked again.

"I think you know what he means, Simmons," Frank fixed his gaze on him. "You admitted you fought with Pa. You said you knocked him out at the barn. You were there."

"Yeah, so?" He took a gulp and downed his drink. "I was there. He promised to pay up and then went back on his word."

"Is that when you killed him?" Ben pressed, as he

leaned forward and drilled into Simmons' eyes.

Simmons' eyes twitched; his face became crimson, and perspiration broke out upon his brow. He cleared his throat nervously and looked each man in the eye. All of Simmons' raw deals, gambling debts, and past lies had caught up with him. Couldn't escape this one.

"We fought like lots of other times. Old man Larue was a mean, ugly fighter and cheater..." he spat. "...and a lousy liar. Don't mean I killed him." He shifted his weight lower in his seat and looked around to see if anyone was listening.

Frank, Ben, and Bob stared at the panicked man across from them. Their plan was working. Time to drill home the question.

"The night we spent in jail, I believe you told me that you didn't know anything about a broken, bloody pitchfork, isn't that right?" Frank asked.

"Yeah, so?"

"How did you know it was broken and bloody? I didn't tell you." Frank was smug.

Simmons hung his head and laughed. The charade was over.

"Whazzit matter now, anyway? Okay. Okay..." he slurped another sip. "Yeah, I went back. Had to get my watch back. Only thing worth getting in that barn."

Now they had him.

Chapter 40 - Time to Go

"We got him, Dol." Ben was all smiles as he came through the door. "He confessed."

"It was almost comical," added Frank. "He thought nothing would happen for a crime committed years ago, so he spilled it all. 'You ain't got nothing on me,' Frank mocked. "Said we couldn't make it hold because we were just talking and he wasn't confessing to anything." Frank chuckled. "You should have seen his face when Bob pulled out the handcuffs."

Dol beamed her approval. "I knew you could do it. Come to the kitchen and get some coffee, and tell me all about it."

"Simmons was so drunk at the time," Ben said with a smirk, "he may not even remember all he told us. Still, his confession holds, because it wasn't coerced. We started out with small talk that led up to LeRoy offering the boys as payment for his debt."

Dol nodded as she leaned in to hear every word. Frank and Ben ping-ponged the story.

"I learned a lot about our father that I didn't want to know, Dol. Simmons claimed to the end that Pa won the pocket watch from him, and that he had only gone back to get it. You remember how ugly Pa got when he was drunk, and how his first reaction was to punch someone," said Frank.

"Simmons said he was angry at your pa for going back on his word," added Ben. "Said he had been promised both boys to work on his farm to pay off LeRoy's debt. That was a deal gone wrong. Simmons played right into our hands."

"Told us when he went back to the barn, Pa was angrier than a whacked hornet's nest." Frank grinned. "I remember seeing that look a few times, don't you, Dol?"

Dol rolled her eyes. She remembered.

"Said Pa looked like he'd already been in a fight. His head was bleeding and there was blood all over his shirt. When Simmons demanded to have his watch back, Pa said he'd lost it. Words escalated, and soon they were in another rumble – this one to the end."

Ben jumped in. "He said your pa grabbed the pitchfork and whacked him so hard, the handle broke in two. A good gash in Simmons' side made him mad enough to attack your pa head on. He lunged for his throat, paying no attention to where the fork lay. When Simmons charged him, LeRoy fell backwards—directly on the tines."

"Then Ben glared at him, Dol." Frank patted Ben

on the back. "You should have seen it. You would have been proud. Ben stood to his feet and said, 'By your own confession, Sy Simmons, you are guilty of manslaughter."

"And then Bob calmly took out his cuffs and put him under arrest for the murder of LeRoy Larue. The look was priceless," grinned Ben. "Priceless."

"Simmons thought we couldn't make it stick, but he confessed in front of three witnesses: the kid he tried to use for child labor, an attorney, and the sheriff of the county. He didn't have a chance," smirked Frank.

"Well," Dol exhaled loudly, "I'm just glad it's done and over. He's going to jail then?"

"To prison – for a long time," said Ben.

Frank's heart filled with jumbled emotions as he packed his bags that night. So much had happened during the past week, it was hard to comprehend. Many questions had been answered, but a lot more had been unearthed.

He wanted to tell Anne his good news about finding Dol, putting his past to rest, and news of Guy and Pa. Ah, yes...and then there was Jenna. What would he tell Anne about her? So much to tell. So much not to tell. It was time to visit Anne at college and have a long talk.

He followed his nose to the aroma of fresh coffee the next morning where Jenna prepared breakfast. When she saw him with his bags, she put the coffee pot down and hurried to his side.

"I hate to see you go, Frank. We were just getting to know each other."

He took her hand and squeezed it. "Dear Jenna, you are such a sweet girl."

She squeezed his hand in return and on impulse, stood on her tiptoes and kissed his cheek. "I will miss you Frank." Her eyes sought his.

"Eww, Jenna," squawked Lizzie as she came into the kitchen, followed by her mother holding Molly in one arm and baby Timothy in the other.

Dol laughed at her daughter. "Jenna's allowed, Lizzie, but she is right. She will miss you, and so will we. We hate to see you go when we just found you. Wish you lived closer. There is still so much to talk about, and I know Jenna would like to get to know you better," she smiled at her friend who looked at the floor. Frank was delighted every time the girl turned a warm red. He cleared his throat, thankful for the interruption.

"My job waits for me back home, but we'll keep in touch, I promise. We must."

Dol agreed. "I will contact Marva Smarkel at the orphanage and let you know if I learn any more information about Josie and Gracie. Hopefully Miss

Smarkel is still serving as Administrator and remembers me. Maybe she will give me some clues about the girls' whereabouts."

"And I will contact the recruiters in Omaha. By his letter, Guy was getting on a ship going out to sea from California. Omaha is the closest place near Tekamah where someone can join the Navy. Maybe they can give me a better lead on Guy's location," said Frank. "In any case, we have each other's phone numbers and addresses now. If anything comes up, we can connect."

How they were going to search for Guy, Josie, and Gracie after that was still a mystery. They knew it had been a miracle the way God brought the two of them back together. They could hope and pray they would find Guy and the girls too. They would continue on their paths and live one day at a time.

No matter what, they knew God had a plan and He always had a perfect way of working things out. They would wait and pray, watch and follow, and somehow...good things would come. They could count on it.

ABOUT THE AUTHOR

C.A. Simonson is an award-winning writer who pens fiction and nonfiction. She has over 200 publications in short stories and articles in anthologies, newspapers, magazines, and online. By writing, she hopes to encourage and inspire, and perhaps get the reader to delve into their own soul for the answer.

The first novel in the Journey Home Series, *Love's Journey Home: The Search for Love*, published in 2013, tells Frank's story of growing from a boy to a man, searching for love and acceptance. It fills in the stories this book alluded to. The third and final book in the series, *Love's Amazing Grace: Reunion* is scheduled for release in the spring of 2016. It will bring all the siblings back together again.

C.A. Simonson is the mother of two grown sons and has six grandchildren. When she is not writing, she loves to craft, play piano, paint, or fish in their backyard pond. She lives in southern Missouri.

Friend her on Facebook:
https://www.facebook.com/CASimonson
Follow on Twitter:
https://twitter.com/candysimonson
Connect on LinkedIn:
http://www.linkedin.com/pub/candace-simonson

Subscribe to blogs at:
http://casimonson.wordpress.com
http://candysimonson.wordpress.com
http://kitchentipsandtreasures.wordpress.com

—COMING SOON—

Love's Amazing Grace: The Reunion, Book III of the Journey Home Series will follow Frank as he tracks clues for Guy on a Navy ship while Dol searches for her two younger sisters.

Guy wonders if he will come home alive from fighting in the South Pacific where atomic bombs are being tested only miles from the ship.

Josie finds her new home hampers her lifestyle in too many ways and seeks her own path. Young Gracie must find the tie that binds them back together again.